World Engine

Standalone Sci-Fi Novels

Paul Haedo

Published by Solan Publishing, 2021.

WORLD ENGINE

First edition. July 20, 2021.

ISBN: 979-8201384517

Written by Paul Haedo.

Also by Paul Haedo

Peacekeeper Series
Peacekeeper: Prequel
Peacekeeper
Rising Tide
Star Rising
Star Destroyer

Proletarian Hearts Series
Proletarian Hearts: Part One

Sci-Fi Box Sets
Sci-Fi Novel Mega Pack: Five Standalone Stories
Peacekeeper: The Complete Series

Standalone Erotic Stories
Innocent Pilgrim

Standalone Literary Novels
Scandinavian Tequila: A Novel

Standalone Poetry Anthologies
Haedian Poetry: Volume One
Moments Are Butterflies: A Poetry Collection

Standalone Religion, Philosophy, and Politics Books
The Communist Republic
A Dalliance Across Thought
The Word Of Era
A Man's Guide To Surviving Marriage In The 21st Century
Marxist-Haedoism
White Assimilation
Peaceful Resistance
The Reality

Standalone Romance Novels
The Director
A Chance Encounter
Beauty Unexpected

Standalone Sci-Fi Novels
Future's Guardian
Journey Home
The Designer
Pulses
World Engine
The Mycelial Invasion
Emily Reed And The Humans

Standalone Sci-Fi Short Story Anthologies
Haedian Sci-Fi Short Stories: Volume One
Haedian Sci-Fi Short Stories: Volume Two

Standalone Self-Help Books
Stack It Tall: A Guide To Writing
Debt Buster: Free Yourself From The Shackles In Less Than A Year

Watch for more at https://books2read.com/ap/n7evX1.

Chapter One

"One more shot, bartender," ordered Captain Nagy, with a tone that conveyed urgency.

"You know you need to walk once you leave, right?" replied the bartender with a smile as he brought the bottle of distilled vodka over.

"I pay you to pour, not to talk," said Captain Nagy, and he pointed at the shot glass. The bartender complied and filled the shot glass to the brim.

"Happy?"

"Very," replied Captain Nagy, and he slid the credits over, enough to pay for the shot and the tip.

"And now I'm happy too," said the bartender with a laugh as he took the credits and went back to cleaning the glasses in preparation for the rush hour shift in a few hours.

The Shiny Moon bar was a miserable little joint, frequented by star traders and veterans with light pockets. The drinks were cheap, the bar stools had holes in the cushions, and the music player whipped up a potent combination of beats mixed with static, the result of corrupted file data that was never fixed or replaced. All in all, a perfect area for a depressed sailor on a mothball salary.

It was not always like this. William Nagy used to be a proud full-time sailor in the Republic of Earth's navy. The main pillar of a heavily corrupt yet still functional republic, the military of Earth could always rely on the greed of representatives and senators. No one ever defunds the military; the pork barrel always has some meat and grease set aside for the brave sons and daughters of the republic, or so people say.

The problem that sailors like William Nagy have run into is quite simple: politicians like to propose bills and projects that revolutionize the republic. Draft a good enough bill and see it implemented across the republic, and you may find yourself in the president's chair. Because of this, you have young and bright-eyed representatives whipping up bills left and right. Even the cranky senators cannot help it; their assistants spend more time theory crafting bills than assisting their bosses in their day-to-day tasks. A mighty republic indeed.

Then came a man by the name of Jonathan Varis. This particular senator thought that he had stumbled on such a gem. It was known as the "Great Reserve," and Jonathan Varis was sure that it was his ticket to the presidency. All the benefits of a standing army and navy, at only a quarter of the price! The plan was simple enough. The soldiers are mothballed on different planets all across the republic; they, in turn, stimulate the local economy by burning through their meager reserve salaries. The sailors are to do the same, only they must remain within an hour's distance of their mothballed vessel, which is moored planetside, guarded by mothballed soldiers who spend more time gambling than patrolling the fence.

Jonathan Varis was right after all; this bill revolutionized society. It helped to lessen the budget deficit, and it gave him the coalition of voters, the perfect blend of deficit hawks and domestic program advocates, to win the presidency. President Varis now governs a republic that is heavily armed, a necessity in modern times, but also a republic that is hesitant in shooting first—the perfect combination for a civilization that wants to negotiate trade deals with other human civilizations across the cosmos.

Captain Nagy heard the shriek of hinges that should have been replaced years ago. An individual had just entered the bar; the sound of the shoe heel was distinct. This particular individual was wearing high heels. Captain Nagy, in an instant, knew exactly who it was.

She walked over to the bar and took a seat next to him. Her dress was the perfect combination of arousal and restraint, perfected down to the last stitch. She, after all, had years of practice in knowing what wins the client over and what does not.

"I think this is the first time that I've seen you here this early," said Captain Nagy with some surprise.

"Slow day," replied the woman with a tone of frustration.

"You never have a slow day," said Captain Nagy in all honesty.

"Tell that to my wallet!"

The bartender walked over to the woman with a smile that concealed a frown. He clearly was not happy at all to see her.

The bartender then asked, "What kind of virgin are we having today?"

"Two virgin Shirley Temples, no ice."

The bartender went over to his bottle collection and fetched the bottle of grenadine. He placed the bottle on the bar counter and fetched two glasses. Pouring a decent portion of grenadine into each glass, he then retrieved the ginger ale from the refrigerator, opened the bottle, and poured its contents into the two glasses until they were almost full. He finally grabbed a spoon, stirred the two liquids together, and slid the finished cocktails over to the woman.

"Just one love; the other is for William," replied the woman, who started to drink her Shirley Temple.

"One virgin Shirley Temple," teased the bartender as he slid the glass over to Captain Nagy.

"I don't want it," he said.

"You've had enough vodka; I like my clients to be sober enough to get hard, at the very least."

"I don't recall purchasing your services, Nicole."

"Then purchase them!"

"What if I just want to sit here and drink my shots, a routine that I was enjoying before you arrived and interrupted it?"

Nicole reached into her purse and pulled out a tightly folded piece of clothing, as well as a pair of handcuffs. She then placed the two items in front of Captain Nagy.

"Is that a Solar Empire officer uniform, female standard dress?"

"Indeed, it is, freshly dry cleaned too."

"She's good," said the bartender with a smile.

Captain Nagy picked up the handcuffs and toyed with them for a moment before placing them back on the bar. He picked up the Shirley Temple that Nicole had purchased for him and drank it all. The vodka had made him quite thirsty, and in only a few moments, his thirst was quenched, and his belly was full and did not want any more liquid. Nicole knew him like a master violinist knows his violin.

"You cleaned the upstairs room?" asked Captain Nagy, looking at the bartender.

"Of course, how long?"

Captain Nagy looked at a smiling Nicole for a moment before replying, "One hour."

"300 credits," replied the bartender, and Captain Nagy counted the chips he had taken from his pocket before sliding them over to the bartender.

"And how much for the rest of that bottle?"

"I'll give it to you for 100 credits," replied the bartender. Captain Nagy slid over a 100-credit chip as the bartender screwed the cap on the bottle and handed it to him.

"And before you say anything, it's for when I get home. Put this on," ordered Captain Nagy, tossing the folded Imperial uniform over to Nicole and handing her the handcuffs as he got up from the barstool, vodka bottle in hand. Nicole paid the bartender for the two drinks as she got up.

"Enjoy yourselves," said the bartender as the two individuals walked over to the corner of the bar and headed up the spiral staircase leading to the lounges and private rooms. Out of sight, the bartender returned to cleaning the glasses in preparation for the rush hour shift that was to come.

Nicole proceeded to put her arm around Captain Nagy's waist as they walked to the rented room. He was wearing his standard reserve uniform, standard naval protocol for enlisted sailors who were not aboard an active ship. Thanks to his reserve status, Captain Nagy was more or less sentenced to wear his reserve dress permanently. He did not mind in the slightest, of course; he had worn a uniform after all for the great majority of his life.

Walking over to the rented room, Nicole drew open the curtains and walked inside. Captain Nagy followed right at her heels as he turned and closed the curtains behind him. There was no door; the room was, after all, designed to facilitate the quick doing of one's business before returning to the bar scene. In pursuit of such a goal, the bed was covered in plastic, which was easily removed and washed between uses. Not the most comfortable of experiences, but neither is inebriated sex, which was the main purpose of said bed.

Nicole wasted no time removing her clothes at lightning speed. She put on the Solar Empire Officer uniform quickly, leaving her naked from the waist down. Laying her purse down, she fumbled through it until she found what she was looking for. It was a small cylindrical device; she turned it on, inserted a tip that she took out from her purse, and walked over to Captain Nagy.

She pulled back his left sleeve and pressed the tip against his forearm, which pierced the skin and drew some blood. The device beeped for a few seconds before letting out a chirp, and a test result then displayed on the screen at the end.

"Not a single venereal disease; I'm impressed," said Nicole.

"Must be all the vodka; nothing can survive in this body," replied Captain Nagy with a smile, shaking the vodka bottle that was still in his hand.

"Give me that," said an annoyed Nicole, who grabbed the bottle and placed it on the floor. "Alright, what do you want today?"

"The usual," replied Captain Nagy as he lay down on the bed.

The bartender continued to clean and polish the glasses in preparation for the flood of workers that would soon descend upon his establishment. To his surprise, he was interrupted by the shrieking sound of his front door hinges. In stepped a man; he was a naval officer, fully dressed in active-duty uniform, and his stripes betrayed him as a Commodore.

"A pleasure, sir. How can I help you?" asked the bartender, surprised to see a senior naval officer in his establishment.

"Captain William Nagy," was his reply.

"You're wondering where you can find him?"

"Yes."

"He's upstairs but occupied at the moment."

"Doing what?"

"Let's just say that he is emptying his ballast tanks," replied the bartender with a joke that had worked on many sailors before.

"I see," said the Commodore, who did not even attempt to modify the resting frown on his face.

"Could I offer you a drink while you wait?"

"That will not be necessary," replied the Commodore, who walked away from the bar and went straight to the spiral staircase at the corner.

"Help yourself to the entire place, you bastard," cursed the bartender to himself as the Commodore walked up the staircase.

He did not need to spend much time deciphering where the person he was searching for was. The squeaking bed was loud enough that one could start to hear it from the middle of the staircase. The Commodore walked over to the room in question, pulled aside the curtains, and he could see Nicole riding hard and fast, like a cowboy fleeing a posse at full gallop.

"I see that the enemy has captured you, Captain," said the Commodore out loud, which startled Nicole. She shrieked briefly and jumped off her client, crossing her legs and throwing down her arms to cover herself as she backed into a corner.

"What the hell are you doing?" hissed Captain Nagy as his session ended.

"I see discipline and respect for rank have faded ever since you were mothballed."

"If you wanted to keep my discipline and respect for rank intact, then maybe you should've kept me on the active-duty payroll."

"Perhaps. Either way, such things are irrelevant now. Admiral Hackett wants to speak with you."

"When?" asked Captain Nagy, who got up from the bed and started to get dressed.

"Immediately. You are to report with me at once."

"I need to pay first," said the Captain plainly.

"Use this to finish your business here; once you are done, meet me outside the bar," replied the Commodore, who pulled out a credit chip and handed it to him before stepping outside.

"Well, it looks like your dry spell today won't be that bad after all," said Captain Nagy with a smile as he handed Nicole the credit chip.

"10,000 credits! Are they mad?" said Nicole with an enormous smile as she took the chip and slipped it at once into her purse.

"Not mad; the navy is just terrible with money. They mothball millions of sailors for years in the name of efficiency, then they overpay for everything else. Either way, that chip buys you for the rest of the day, does it not?"

"I suppose it does," replied Nicole with a smile.

"In that case, bring this vodka bottle to my apartment and wait there until I return. I'm sure you know the address?" said Captain Nagy, who handed her the bottle and his apartment key.

"Of course. I've been there so many times that I sometimes dream inside that apartment."

"That's the spirit! Wait for me there," said Captain Nagy, and he walked out once he finished getting dressed.

Captain Nagy made his way down the staircase and waved goodbye to the bartender as he left the bar. He was quite dizzy, a result of the several shots that he had enjoyed previously, but he could still more or less walk without falling over.

"An absolute travesty; your current state is an insult to the navy," hissed the Commodore, who was waiting for him.

"I'm mothballed. Until you give me my commission back, I'm not even in the navy for all intents and purposes," retorted the Captain.

"Follow me, Captain," ordered the Commodore, and the pair started to walk down the street.

The Commodore pulled out his personal computer and called for his aircraft. It was waiting overhead; the pilot wasted no time in descending and then landing right in the middle of the street.

"I believe that breaks a few traffic laws," said Captain Nagy with a grin.

"Get in," ordered the Commodore, and Captain Nagy wasted no time in doing so. He could see Nicole leave the bar just as the aircraft began to take off; they exchanged waves as the aircraft ascended and then sped off.

"Lovely girl. She makes for a terrible Imperial officer; on the other hand, the Solar Empire is much less pleasant in their interrogations," added the Commodore, whose face betrayed a smile.

"That is more or less the idea in having her wear it."

Chapter Two

The Commodore and the Captain did not speak for the rest of the trip. It did not take long to arrive at their destination; after all, the Admiralty for the 89th reserve fleet, which was the fleet that Captain Nagy's ship was assigned to, was within an hour or so of Captain Nagy's apartment by public transportation. By air, the trip took less than ten minutes, and the journey from The Shiny Moon bar to the Admiralty building felt like a blink of time.

The aircraft descended and landed, and the two men stepped off. The pilot reclined the seat back and rested, wasting no time taking a break as the Commodore and the Captain left the landing pad and entered the building. Inside was a small room, with two sentry soldiers standing next to a metallic door. The Commodore walked up to the retina scanner, and Captain Nagy did the same. It cleared both men, and the doors opened.

The building inside was richly decorated and exquisite in its cleanliness. A naval secretary smiled and got up to greet them as they walked the hallway that connected the metallic security door with the lobby. The secretary met the two men right as they entered the lobby, which was covered with polished marble and many different flags.

"A pleasure. How can I help you two?" asked the secretary, her voice the perfect combination of kindness and quickness.

"We are here to see Admiral Hackett," replied the Commodore.

"I'll let the Admiral know that you have arrived. Please take a seat while you wait," said the secretary, who pointed to a row of chairs in the right corner of the room. The two men took a seat as the secretary returned to her desk and phoned the Admiral's office, letting him know that his expected guests had arrived.

The Captain and the Commodore waited for several minutes until the secretary's phone rang. She picked it up with great speed, and after a brief conversation, she hung up.

She got up before saying, "The Admiral will see you now. With me, please." She waited until the two men got up and walked over to her before proceeding to escort them to Admiral Hackett's office.

The hallways of the Admiralty building continued with lavish decorations. Flag after flag was prominently displayed; some of the flags represented distinct ships that had earned high praise and rewards, while others denoted different campaigns in which the 89th participated before the entire fleet was demoted to reserve status. Even though the fleet was currently mothballed all across the Sol system, with the majority of the cruisers slowly rotting on Earth proper, it was one of the most decorated fleets in the entire Republican Navy. An impressive feat for the mother civilization that still clings to the ideals of a republic.

The three individuals continued to walk the hallway until they at long last reached the Admiral's office. The secretary opened the door and held it open for the Captain and the Commodore, closing it behind them as they entered. The Admiral's office was spacious and very well decorated with flags, medals, and other naval memorabilia that one accumulates after decades of service. Such was the office of Admiral Hackett, leader of the 89th reserve fleet, once upon a time one of the greatest strategic minds in the entire Republican Navy.

"A pleasure and honor, sir," said Captain Nagy, who walked up to the seated Admiral and saluted at attention.

"A pleasure as well, Captain. Please take a seat, the both of you," ordered Admiral Hackett, and both the Commodore and the Captain took a seat in the two chairs in front of the Admiral's desk.

"You look out of place in that dress."

"I agree completely. I would rather wear active-duty dress; then again, our glorious republic had other plans for me, sir."

"Indeed, one of the most decorated fleets in our navy, mothballed and left to rot across our home system. Anyway, I am here to try and rectify such an error, starting with you."

"You're reinstating my commission?"

"Indeed, your cruiser is coming out of mothball."

Captain Nagy already had a strong feeling that he was going to be reinstated—sending the Commodore to hunt him down, overpaying severely to ensure that he finished his business quickly with Nicole, all were obvious signs. The Republican Navy does not lift a finger after all without a purpose. And doing all of that meant that he was needed for something. Yet what that something was, he did not know.

"Sir, if I may ask a blunt question."

"You may, and if I get offended, I'll blame the alcohol that courses through your veins," replied Admiral Hackett with a smile, who clearly saw the less-than-perfect gait of Captain Nagy as he walked into his office.

"I appreciate that, sir. You sent this Commodore here on a personal mission, direct from your hand; did you not?"

"I did," replied Admiral Hackett, who was intrigued by this line of questioning.

"Why didn't you have some official messengers track me down? Using a Commodore to hunt down an old Captain whose best service years are behind him does not seem like the best use of fleet resources."

"No, but circumstance demands it," replied Admiral Hackett, who got up and walked over to his liquor cabinet.

"Circumstance?"

"Are you a bourbon man by any chance, William?" asked Admiral Hackett, who broke two simultaneous regulations: addressing a subordinate by their first name and offering alcohol to a subordinate.

"I am now, sir," replied Captain Nagy, who never refused a drink.

"I'll have to carry him out at this rate, sir," added the Commodore with a jest.

"I'm sure he'll sober up by the time he leaves my office. Say, Captain, how's the liver?" asked Admiral Hackett, who walked over with two glasses of bourbon on the rocks, handing one of them to Captain Nagy.

"More or less half-dead by this point. Cheers, sir," replied Captain Nagy, and he lifted his glass. The Admiral reciprocated; the two glasses clinked.

The Admiral walked back to his chair and sat down. Smelling and tasting the bourbon before taking a sip, he eyed the subordinate in front of him as he drank the bourbon like a kid drinks fruit juice. He could not help it; he smiled and let out a laugh.

"Well, your ship's doctor will have to give you a physical before I can clear you for departure, once you're briefed, of course," said Admiral Hackett. Captain Nagy stopped drinking as the topic of his old ship came up.

"How's the old girl?"

"In the same condition as the rest of my fleet: abyssal compared to the days when she roamed the stars."

"Any retrofits or improvements since the initial mothball?"

"Not a single one. Every year she got a cleaning and a checkup, but not much else. Assuming the cleaning crews did not doctor their schedules, of course. For all I know, the ship hasn't been touched in over a decade," replied the Admiral, who did not like the words that came out of his mouth.

"Damn the politicians; damn them all."

"Well, I hope the bourbon went down well at the very least."

"It did; I thank you for it," replied Captain Nagy, who finished up the last drops of bourbon and set the empty glass with ice down on the Admiral's desk.

"Now to the business at hand: you need to be briefed. Commodore, mind fetching the dossier?" ordered Admiral Hackett, and the Commodore got up and briskly walked out of the office in pursuit of his orders.

"Give him a moment to get the papers. In the meantime, how has the last decade of reserve status treated you?"

"Abysmally, sir."

"Free time proved to be too great of a foe to best?"

"It wasn't the fact that I had nothing to do; the problem, sir, was the depression of morale. I saw the same faces, attached to men who used to be officers and soldiers. They gave away years and years, riding the void of space on metallic boxes, only to be treated as an expenditure that should be cut as much as possible. The President does not have the same 89th that his predecessors had; I can say that right now with absolute certainty."

"No, he does not; not by a long shot," said Admiral Hackett. The Commodore arrived just as the Admiral finished his words.

"Perfect. Please read up, Captain, and do not hesitate to ask questions," ordered the Admiral as the Commodore handed Captain Nagy the dossier folder.

Captain Nagy read the folder for a good fifteen minutes, and he read it several times. From an observer's viewpoint, one could assume that the more he read it, the more he struggled to understand. Finally, he could not take it anymore.

"No, it doesn't exist," said Captain Nagy with full certainty in his voice.

"You certain of that?" replied Admiral Hackett, who reclined in his chair.

"Sir, the Terraforming Installation is a myth, a rumor, a tale that the idiot ensigns tell themselves to pass the time. You're ordering me to find it; how can I find something for you that does not exist?"

The Admiral pulled out a drawer and took out a full-service marine battle rifle. He looked at the Commodore and said, "Sierra protocol, I'll knock three times on the door to disengage." The Admiral handed the rifle to the Commodore, who immediately got up.

"Yes, sir," he replied, and walked outside of the office, closing the door shut behind him. He stood directly in front of the door, in the same sentry stance that Captain Nagy saw the two sentries in before entering the Admiralty building.

"Sierra protocol?" asked Captain Nagy, who tried to contain his laughter.

"When you spend ten years without a single thing to do, you create fun little protocols. It's the best Do-Not-Disturb sign in the galaxy," replied the Admiral with a laugh; Captain Nagy joined in.

"I suppose it is," added Captain Nagy in between chuckles.

"Alright, William, back to the business at hand. Just a second," said the Admiral as he got up and walked towards one of the paintings on the wall.

He slid it over, revealing a safe, and typed in a code that unlocked it. There were many stacks of papers and folders, no doubt containing priceless and highly classified secrets. He pulled out the folder that was on top of the pile and walked over to a seated Captain Nagy, handing him the folder.

The style was unmistakable; this was a Solar Empire dossier. The contents were clearly translated from their language, but the information was still just as shocking.

"Where did we get this?" asked Captain Nagy with astonishment.

"The idiots over at Clandestine Intelligence; for once in their miserable lives, they actually did something useful."

"And we can verify its accuracy?"

"With a high degree of certainty, yes."

Captain Nagy continued to skim through the dossier, reading each piece of information it contained over and over. Dozens of perfectly terraformed worlds located in very remote areas of the galaxy. Organic-based lifeforms with DNA that matches that of Earth-origin species. Orbits are perfectly in the middle of each star's Goldilocks zone; gravity on each world was more or less 1g. The Solar Empire believes, Admiral Hackett believes, but Captain Nagy still needs convincing.

"You want me to take the ship out 'clandestinely,' don't you, sir?"

"Even a decade of drinking did not dull your intelligence. Yes, this mission is not an official one. I am going to be frank with you, Captain: I am bored out of my mind, and the politicians will not lift a finger to take my fleet out of mothball. You are going to be my bait, the thing that wakes up those fat-cat politicians and makes them pounce on my suggestions. Your ship is a rust bucket, using decades-old gear and tech, perfect for slipping under the radar and avoiding suspicion from every single spy stationed on the frontier worlds. I want you to hunt down these leads, confirm the existence of the Terraforming Installation, and then immediately relay said confirmation to me."

"Once the Republic discovers the existence of the Terraforming Installation, they'll have no choice but to bring out the entire reserve wing of the navy and army from mothball. The entire galaxy will scramble to war in order to capture it. Indeed, whoever obtains such a valuable asset as the Terraforming Installation controls the fate of every single human civilization in the universe. The power to make any solar system a habitable one; the implications are just unfathomable," said Captain Nagy, his mind racing with the potential implications of such technology existing in the universe.

"I don't want you back until you find that Terraforming Installation. I'm giving you full control over your crew and a complete pardon from any regulations that you may break as you assemble said crew. Fill up your cruiser with the scum of the frontier if you so choose. All I care about is confirmation from you regarding the Terraforming Installation once you find it," ordered Admiral Hackett. Captain Nagy got up and placed the dossier on the Admiral's desk as he leaned in.

"Have the dossier sent to the safe in my captain's quarters, assuming they did not take it out in the past decade. One last thing, sir: what is the scuttle protocol for this mission?"

"Any risk of capture or failure during the mission, self-destruct with all hands aboard."

"Understood, sir. Mind if I borrow the Commodore's aircraft to help me in hunting down my old crew and recruiting new individuals?"

"Of course, the aircraft is yours. I'll make sure to get this dossier into your safe. Give me 24 hours at the minimum to get your ship out of mothball; your engineers will have to get her up to 100% on their own as you depart Sol, but you'll be FTL-capable at the bare minimum," replied Admiral Hackett, who picked up the dossier on his desk as he got up from his chair.

The Admiral and the Captain walked over to the door of the Admiral's office. The Admiral knocked three times on the door, disengaging the 'Sierra protocol' that had been activated a few moments previously. The Commodore turned around and opened the door, holding it open for the Admiral and Captain as they stepped outside the office.

"Good luck, officer," said Admiral Hackett, extending his arm and shaking Captain Nagy's hand with a firm grasp.

"Thank you, sir," replied Captain Nagy. The three men separated; Captain Nagy turned left and walked back to the lobby, while the Admiral and Commodore turned right and continued to walk deeper into the Admiralty building.

The captain returned to the lobby after a brief walk and was greeted by the secretary as he left the Admiralty building. With the metal door sealing shut behind him, he stepped outside and walked to the aircraft, where the pilot inside was still enjoying his break from flying. The captain walked right up to the window and tapped it a few times with his knuckles to snap the pilot to attention. He then entered the aircraft through one of the rear doors.

"You've been assigned to me, pilot; I have several errands to run for the Admiral," ordered Captain Nagy.

"One second, sir, while I confirm with the Commodore," replied the pilot, who for a few moments contacted the Commodore and requested authorization for the command transfer.

"The Commodore confirms your order transfer. Where to first, sir?" asked the pilot, and Captain Nagy gave him the street where his apartment was located.

"Roger, sir, we'll be there momentarily. Want me to hover overhead and wait for you, or will you require more time to complete your errand?" asked the pilot as he turned on the aircraft and prepared for takeoff.

"Set it to loop around on autopilot and return to your relaxation. I'll message you once I'm done and ready for pickup."

"Understood, sir. My communicator code is 84645-78-10283; message that address with your personal computer once you're ready," said the pilot as he lifted off from the Admiralty building. Captain Nagy made sure to record the code in his personal computer before he forgot.

The ride was quick, around ten minutes, all thanks to the naval policy of having the mothballed crew of a starship remain within an hour's distance of the mothballed vessel. Captain Nagy was fortunate; his ship was mothballed in one of the main reserve shipyards on Earth, which meant that his one-hour circle was nestled in one of the great metropolitan cities on Earth. A great place to be in order to live out one's reserve status life, a nightmare when you need to get the old crew back together.

Captain Nagy searched for a few minutes until he found the now-ancient group chat on his personal computer. He knew that the contact numbers would still be accurate; all reservists are mandated to retain the same communication numbers in the event that they are reactivated to active duty. He typed out the sentence he had waited to type for over a decade: "The Shiny Moon is shining brighter than the sun." He followed that sentence with: "Crew, report to active stations."

The message went out, and for just over a thousand men, as well as a few women, their lives of mindless muddling about had come to an end. A few seconds after the message was sent out, Captain Nagy began to receive notifications that the order was confirmed and being carried out by several crew members. Smiling, he silenced his personal computer and returned it to his pocket. Looking at his reserve status uniform, he uttered to himself, "I'm going to have to polish the old suit before I talk to the first officer."

"Alright, sir, we're approaching the designation. Want me to drop you off on the street? There's little traffic from the looks of it."

"Sounds good, drop us down, pilot."

Chapter Three

The pilot slowed down and started to bring the aircraft down towards the surface. It landed in the middle of the street; there was no traffic on either end, but all of the pedestrians stopped to look at the strange sight. Captain Nagy stepped out of the aircraft and onto the street, and once the pedestrians saw that it was a military aircraft, everyone continued whatever they had been doing beforehand.

Captain Nagy started to walk towards the door of his apartment complex, and the pilot lifted off right as he reached the door handles. He opened the door and smiled at the civilians who stared at him with eyes of disapproval. Ignoring them after the initial smile, he walked up the staircase towards the 4th floor, and once he arrived at the floor, he entered the hallway and began to make his way towards his apartment, where he hoped that Nicole would be waiting. Captain Nagy was planning to see just how far Admiral Hackett's free reign in allowing him to choose his own crew could be stretched before it broke.

He arrived at his apartment and reached into his pocket to get the key. He stumbled for a moment because he did not find it. Frustrated that he must have forgotten it, he quickly remembered that he had given the key, as well as the purchased vodka bottle, to Nicole before leaving The Shiny Moon bar with the Commodore. Smiling at his forgetfulness, he knocked on the door to his own apartment.

"Who is it?" said a voice that Captain Nagy was all too familiar with.

"A poor captain in search of his love and vodka bottle."

He heard the door unlock, and immediately he was greeted by Nicole, who was wearing just a bath towel.

"I see you took a shower," said Captain Nagy as he entered his apartment, closing and locking the door behind him.

"Your apartment is spartan in, well, just about everything. I decided to pass the time by showering until the water started to run cold."

"I have no problem with that; anyway, I wanted to run something by you."

"It'll have to wait. First, we need to conclude our previous business," replied Nicole, and she led the captain to his bed and began to remove his clothes with some force.

"Looks like that shower was to cool off your steam more than anything else," teased Captain Nagy, who helped Nicole remove his reserve uniform until he was naked.

Nicole pushed Captain Nagy onto the bed and then removed the bath towel she was wearing. She wasted no time; she leaned over and began to stroke the captain's penis until it was erect. Once it was erect, she climbed on top of him, lowered herself onto him, and began to ride.

"You keep moving like that, and we are going to conclude quite soon," moaned the captain after a moment, as Nicole showed no mercy with her hips.

"That's the idea, sweetie," replied Nicole with a smile, and she simultaneously squeezed her vaginal muscles while increasing the speed of her ride.

The captain did not lie; after a few minutes, he grunted in joy as his penis twitched inside Nicole. Nicole expertly rocked her hips slowly for a few moments before peeling off the captain.

"You mentioned that you had something you wanted to run by me?" asked Nicole, looking at a captain who clearly lacked endurance.

"Ah yes, I may be wrong, but if I remember correctly, you told me a few months back that you work for a guild of sex workers, is that correct?" asked the captain, who was somewhat out of breath.

"Yes, although I'll be hurt if you think that I wasn't good enough just now," replied Nicole with a smile.

"Do not worry, my love, you were more than good. Anyway, I have been reinstated; The Shiny Moon and her crew are coming out of mothball."

"That's terrific news! Although it means that this will no doubt be our last session for quite some time."

"Not necessarily. You see, I need a full civilian crew roster, and considering the mission that we have been assigned, I have an ingenious idea."

"Let's hear this idea of yours, William."

"The civilian crew roster is in charge of assisting the crew with janitorial duties, maintenance, and other miscellaneous tasks that we can't exactly handle. Normally, they are hired out on contract, and every few months, we need to stop on a random world as the vast majority of them decide not to renew their enlistment. Many of them use the enlistment as a way to settle on a frontier world and earn some money to start a new life there. Either way, our mission does not give me such an opportunity."

"Hmm, and I know of a solution to this problem?"

"You bet you do. I want to fill the entirety of the civilian roster with working girls. Knowing the state of our republic's glorious navy, especially the likely state of my crew after suffering mothball for a decade, the mission is going to fail if they cannot keep their sexual urges and desires in check. We need enough girls that their base instincts can be sated aboard the vessel. Shore leave is going to be in the bunk bed each night for several years if we get unlucky. You've been in the business for a long time; I have no doubt that you can get a thousand girls who are down on their luck to consider enlisting," replied the captain. Nicole immediately got up from the bed and started to pace around the apartment bedroom.

"That is crazy. What about the regulations? Whenever we sex workers poke our noses near the shipyards, we get chased off by the guards. And prostitution aboard a naval ship is still forbidden."

"Let us just say I have a free hand in choosing my crew, straight from one of the admirals. While he is likely to curse me out once he discovers the number of civilian sex workers that I am enlisting, you all will be in the clear. Think about it: over a thousand sailors who are horny up to their eyeballs, locked inside bulkheads with little shore leave. You'll get paid as a civilian contractor, plus any services that you provide."

"It's crazy, but then again, you always were one of the wildest sailors that I ever had the pleasure of working for. And you are in luck; I think I can get you the number of girls that you seek for your ship," replied Nicole, who walked back to the bed and cuddled next to the captain.

"Tell me more," asked the captain, kissing Nicole's left brow.

"The guild is kicking me and all the older girls out. Once you start to reach your mid-thirties, you are considered to be used goods in this business. You make a bunch of money when you are young; if you are smart and save most of it, you can retire from just a decade of working in your twenties. I no longer get any guild jobs, and I likely have only a year or two remaining before the guild cuts me off for failure to pay my dues," replied Nicole, who was clearly frustrated with the entire affair.

"That's why today was a slow day for you, and why you sought me out at The Shiny Moon bar. You aren't getting any work."

"Exactly, William. They can't just kick us out because we are old; we'd sue the guild until they go bankrupt for age discrimination, but they have all the power to 'allocate jobs according to customer demand' and then kick us out when we can't pay the member dues."

"How many girls are going to be affected?"

"Just over a thousand. I swear today is the day of fortunes for all the unfortunates."

"Indeed."

"Just one thing: you mentioned just a short while ago that The Shiny Moon was coming out of mothball, that's the name of your ship?"

"Aye; she's old, but still beautiful," replied the captain, kissing Nicole again on the brow. She smiled deeply and responded with a kiss of her own.

"No wonder you frequent that bar so often."

"Ah, that reminds me, I need to speak to the owner of that bar again. No doubt he's working the rush hour shift by now."

"Why?"

"Because he will soon be your first officer."

"You're kidding! How many times has he mocked, jested, and tormented you over the years? And that's just the times that I was there to witness it! He's your second in command?" asked Nicole in astonishment.

"That is the role of a first officer: to make sure that the captain of the vessel remains fit for as long as possible."

"And the politicians have the gall to say that we sex workers are manipulating our clients," scoffed Nicole as Captain Nagy got up and walked over to his closet.

"Where are you going?" asked Nicole as Captain Nagy opened the closet door and pulled out his active-duty uniform.

"These things are a pain in the ass to get up to protocol. Mind giving me a hand?"

"Gladly," giggled Nicole, and she got up to help him.

It was an ordeal that took over ten minutes, but it was finally done. The uniform was up to code, and the captain could not help the mighty thrill of shakes he experienced as he saw himself in his old uniform for the first time in over ten years. A man in his late forties, the uniform squeezed him in many different places, the result of his wildly out-of-shape body.

"You are going to need a new size," suggested Nicole.

"No, I'm going to exercise and starve myself down. Knowing the first officer, I'll be back to my thirty-year-old self in three weeks," replied the captain with a chuckle as he slowly paced around the apartment bedroom, trying to acclimate himself to the tight fit of his uniform.

"Alright, you go talk to your first officer. I'll stay in your apartment and make a few hundred calls to a bunch of people. I think I'll have a thousand girls willing to enlist by tomorrow," said Nicole as she walked with the captain to the apartment door.

Unlocking the door, he opened it and kissed Nicole goodbye as he closed it behind him. He could hear Nicole locking the door, and the captain began to make his way through the floor and towards the staircase. Once he reached the staircase, he pulled out his personal computer and messaged the pilot that he would soon be out. Putting the personal computer away, the captain started to walk down the stairs, a feat that was made very difficult by the uniform that was compressing his body like a corset.

Slowly making his way down the stairs, he stepped outside and found that the pilot had already landed the aircraft. With annoyed pedestrians staring at him, especially at his uneven gait, he made his way to the aircraft and entered through one of the back doors.

"A pleasure to see you again, sir. Where to next?"

"I'll message you the address," replied Captain Nagy, and he messaged the pilot's communicator the address of The Shiny Moon bar.

"We'll be there shortly, sir," said the pilot, taking off quickly once the destination was confirmed.

The pilot accelerated the aircraft and zipped through the city. Since the bar was within walking distance of the captain's apartment, the aircraft only needed to zip past a few blocks and buildings before it hovered over the street next to the bar. The pilot lowered the aircraft and landed it on the street, the traffic being more or less non-existent, the same as the street adjacent to the captain's apartment. The whole affair took less than two minutes.

"I shouldn't be too long," Captain Nagy said to the pilot as he stepped outside of the aircraft and onto the street.

Captain Nagy started to walk towards the entrance of The Shiny Moon bar. The pilot lifted off behind him, and the aircraft went out of sight right as the captain reached the entrance to the bar. He pushed the door, and the hinges shrieked as the door swung open. He walked inside in search of the bartender.

The bar was more active than it had been just half an hour ago. A few patrons were scattered throughout the bar, some enjoying themselves with a game of pool, a few talked with bottles in hand at the far corners, and a few were seated at the bar. There was still some time before rush hour, but already The Shiny Moon bar was picking up activity.

Captain Nagy, dressed in a clean active-duty uniform that had been begging to be worn for a decade, walked through the bar. The uniform, even at a distance, was several sizes too small for the body that the captain now possessed, and his uneven gait turned several heads as he made his way to one of the open bar stools.

The bartender already knew the topic of conversation that was to come; he had, after all, received the same message as the entire crew of the Shiny Moon. He was busy at the moment, serving drinks to the bar patrons, so the captain took a seat at one of the open bar stools and waited until he finally had the attention of the bartender.

"What can I get you, Captain?" asked the bartender, smiling as he saw his old boss in active-duty uniform.

"The coldest water that you can get me."

The bartender opened the fridge and gave the captain a glass bottle of water, the highest quality that he had available. The captain screwed the cap open and began to gulp it down.

"The vodka giving you the blues, sir?"

"It was; now it's better. Thank you, First Officer."

"Glad to hear it. Just a second, sir." The First Officer left the bar and went to the kitchen. A faint, brisk, and inaudible conversation could be heard, and a few moments later, the First Officer emerged from the kitchen, accompanied by a young man.

The First Officer took out the keys to the bar from his pocket and handed them to the young man. The young man's eyes widened, knowing that the time had come for him to take over the establishment. The captain stared attentively as he continued to drink his water; he had never seen the kid before; if he had, he had long forgotten the moment.

"The bar's yours now, nephew. Remember my advice: burn half the profits in fun, save the other half for the days when trouble arrives. Enjoy your life if I don't see you again," said the First Officer, who was clearly not good at farewells.

"I will, Uncle. Thank you for everything," said the First Officer's nephew, and the two hugged, with the First Officer tapping his nephew's back shoulder. Once the embrace had ended, the First Officer stepped out from behind the bar and walked over to his captain.

"Give me ten or so minutes to change into my old active-duty dress. Seeing your current uniform, it looks like I'm going to have a great time wearing it," said the First Officer as he walked away from the bar, made his way up the spiral staircase to the second floor, and then quickly disappeared from view.

"It is an honor to meet you, sir. My uncle has told me many stories about the Shiny Moon from back in the day," said the new bartender.

"Those times don't exist anymore," replied the captain grimly.

"Perhaps, sir, but that does not mean that such times cannot exist again. Anyway, let me know if I can get you anything else," said the bartender as he got to work on serving his other customers.

The first officer did not lie; around ten or so minutes had passed before the captain saw him again. He walked slowly yet proudly; even from the second floor, one could see from a distance that the uniform was simply not the correct size for his present body. He made his way down the spiral staircase, walked over to the captain, and saluted.

"Ready to head underway, sir?" asked the first officer.

"I've been ready for ten years, first officer. Let's go," replied the captain, and the two men walked out of the bar.

They stood at the entrance as the captain messaged the pilot to descend. After half a minute or so of waiting, the pilot descended and landed in the middle of the street. The two men walked to the aircraft.

"Is it possible for the military to teach its people how to use a damn automobile instead of parking your aircraft wherever you goddamn please?" yelled a pedestrian heckler from behind them.

The two men ignored the jab and entered the aircraft.

"You don't even get a response from them. Useless and worthless, the whole lot of..." The heckler's comments were silenced by the closing of the aircraft door, which soundproofed the cabin from outside noise.

"Where to now, sir?" asked the pilot, who slowly ascended the aircraft as he waited for a new destination.

"Hold the aircraft for a moment while I figure out just that," replied the captain as he took out his personal computer.

"Roger that, sir."

The captain messaged the personal computer of Nicole, asking her how the recruitment of the civilian sex workers was coming along. Nicole messaged him back, saying that it was going well, and she then asked the captain how the meeting with the first officer went. He messaged back, saying that it went well and that they were currently heading to the apartment to discuss further details regarding the mission. The captain also asked Nicole to wait for them there. She replied, confirming the previous message.

"Take the both of us back to the apartment complex from which we had just come. And to prevent the civilians from complaining a second longer, land on the roof, and we'll make our way down," ordered the captain.

"At once, sir," replied the pilot, and he started to fly the aircraft toward Captain Nagy's apartment complex.

It was a quick journey; it took more or less the same amount of time as the previous trip from the apartment to the bar. The pilot descended and looked around the roof for a landing spot.

"Sir, there is no landing spot large enough on this roof that will allow us to land safely," said the pilot.

"Screw the civilians, Captain; I say we land on the street," suggested the first officer.

"You're my first officer again after a decade, and in just a few minutes, you are already giving good advice. Pilot, follow the suggestion that the first officer just gave."

"Right away, sir," replied the pilot, and he landed on the street.

Chapter Four

The two men opened the door and left the aircraft; the pilot then ascended and left as the two men walked toward the apartment complex door. They entered the apartment building and walked up the staircase until they reached the fourth door, then walked to the captain's apartment. Once there, the captain knocked on his apartment door.

"Yes?" asked the voice of Nicole from the other side.

"A captain and his first officer are here to make your acquaintance," replied Captain Nagy.

"Two at the same time? Must be my lucky day," joked Nicole, and she unlocked the door. She held it open until the two men walked inside, and then she closed and locked the door behind her.

"In ten years, I've never been to your Earthside captain's quarters. It looks as bland as the one aboard the Shiny Moon," added the first officer.

"Blame the amount of money that I spent patronizing your bar," replied the captain.

"I think the only one who is to blame is you, my dear," added Nicole.

"Oh, how supportive of you," hissed the captain.

"You're the captain; there's no one higher up the chain of ship command that you can blame other than yourself. In addition, all that alcohol was money that you could have otherwise spent on me," retorted Nicole as she walked to the couch and took a seat.

The captain and the first officer of the Shiny Moon followed her example until the three of them were seated in the living room area of the apartment. The two men 'pulsed' during each breath; the tight-fitting uniforms looked like tightly wrapped cocoons that squeezed their bodies as they took in each and every breath.

"The both of you need to get new uniforms. A child wouldn't respect you if they saw you like this; how can your crew be expected to do so?"

She was wearing one of the captain's supplementary reserve status uniforms, both the shirt and pants. She, however, was barefoot—a clothing combination that no doubt confused the first officer, who stared at her in the same way that an owl stares at an interesting creature.

"Captain, who is she?"

"Head of the civilian crew, for all intents and purposes."

"I see," replied the first officer, who was still perplexed.

"Speaking of my civilian crew, how goes your initial recruitment?" asked the captain, who turned to face Nicole.

"Very well, at around the level that I initially suspected. While a few of the girls refused, I would say a good 93% of the girls that I have talked to have agreed to enlist for one enlistment of six months. I, alongside a few of the girls who have decided to help with recruiting, have informed them that in the event of the mission continuing for more than six months, they'll be entitled to double the contract pay as per naval contract extension policies."

"And all of this you did in thirty or so minutes? Impressive."

"Well, it's not exactly difficult to convince them. Do you want to make money through a civilian military service enlistment, as well as mountains of money banging all the horny sailors who cannot go anywhere other than you for their sexual needs? And finally, get a chance to finish the contract on some fresh frontier world with endless career potential? Or do you want to stay on Earth, get fired in a few years, and live the rest of your days in horrid poverty? Which option do you think most of them will go for?"

"The first one."

"There's your answer."

"I'm somewhat ignorant as to the civilian recruitment policy nowadays, but I do not believe there will be any 'banging' of the horny sailors," said the first officer matter-of-factly.

"That reminds me, I need to fill you in on a few things, first officer."

"Like what?"

"Well, for one, the near entirety of our civilian roster, for the most part, is going to be female sex workers. Assuming Nicole here gets the necessary numbers, which judging by her update she will likely have no problem doing, this gives us an even gender ratio of 50/50. You know how difficult it is to get such a balanced ratio in our navy?" replied the captain, who said the last sentence of his response with some amusement and pride.

"Sir, are you insane?" asked the first officer, who could not believe what he was hearing.

"Not really, no."

"How many prostitutes are we talking about, civilian?" asked the first officer, looking directly at Nicole.

"If I'm lucky, around a thousand or so; if I'm really lucky, perhaps..." Nicole was interrupted by the first officer.

"ONE FUCKING THOUSAND!" yelled the first officer, whose shock overrode his discipline.

"Times are tough, and the old crew that we used to enjoy ironclad discipline from is more or less half dead from a decade of mothball at this point. I have a plan to make it work," added the captain, who was enjoying this incredibly rare moment, a moment that will likely never repeat again.

"Do tell," said the first officer.

"Simple: our discipline is going to be abysmal, and the nature of our mission, which I got directly from the Admiral's mouth, means we need to sober up from a decade of hell in a few hours' time. Since our crew is more feral beasts than men at this point, we need to detoxify them with the only vice that will be safe to allow on board, at least once the medical team checks us all for venereal diseases and eradicates them."

"And what about the regulations against sexual activity aboard a naval vessel? You remember the drama when that chef was dating that sensor team ensign during her off-duty hours? Morale was shot aboard ship for weeks."

"What was the gender ratio aboard ship during this time?" asked Nicole.

"How is that at all relevant to this discussion?" replied the first officer.

"Answer my question, and you'll find out," pressed Nicole.

"I think there were no more than a dozen female sailors aboard the vessel; one of them was on the bridge for whatever reason," replied the captain.

"Theresa, if I recall correctly," added the first officer.

"Indeed, always asking me if I wanted coffee," replied the captain, smiling as the nostalgia came to him.

"So, 99% men was the ratio, and you're wondering why 'morale' was shot when word got around that one lucky bastard in a thousand got to spend some alone time with a woman. You men are incredibly foolish; our species spans the galaxy, and yet we still think that excluding half the species aboard a space vessel helps with efficiency and morale," added Nicole.

"Without restraint of sexual relations aboard a vessel, the unity of the crew will be shattered by jealousy and petty gossip intrigue," replied the first officer.

"He still does not see it," remarked Nicole, looking at the captain.

"To be fair, I don't see it either," replied the captain in defense of his first officer.

"When men get too much sex, they complain that it is too easy to get. When they get too little sex, they complain that it is too hard to get. When they get an average amount, they complain that they do not get it often enough. How about the general consensus settling around getting all the sex that one could want and enjoying the fact that the pleasurable activity is as common as the air that we breathe? Wouldn't that be a galaxy that is nice to live in?"

"I still don't see how that pertains to the discussion at hand," said the first officer.

"When the captain first proposed this plan to me, I thought that it was crazy, but I've grown to like it in the thirty minutes that I've so far spent helping to implement it. Your crew, according to the captain, will be around a thousand sailors; is that correct?"

"Yes, the general sailor complement, excluding the civilians, is around a thousand. Including the civilians, the number of personnel aboard is around two thousand, the standard crew complement for a naval cruiser of our republic."

"Perfect, a thousand sailors, which for the absolute most part are male for stupid reasons that we are not going to get into. A thousand civilian worker women gives you a gender ratio of 50/50, a good thing according to your captain, and a statement that I also agree with. Because the ratio is balanced, and especially because both the men, by nature of their current status and respective employment, and the women, by nature of their current status and respective employment, are eager to engage in sexual intercourse, all your problems fade away. Your sailors are happy, the civilian workers are happy, your ship runs smoothly, which means you are happy. Everyone is happy."

"Did you run this 'ingenious' idea by the Admiral, Captain?"

"Nope, I will run it by him eventually."

"And the regulations that this ingenious plan breaks?"

"The Admiral gave me permission to choose the civilian part of the ship roster as I see fit. He even said that he does not mind if I fill the ship with the scum of the frontier; all he cares about is our success in the mission that he has taken us out of mothball to do."

"I really want to hear what this mission is."

"I'll let you and the rest of the officers know during the first briefing we have as we depart Sol."

"Alright, looks like we've covered everything. Does anyone have anything else to add?" asked Nicole.

"No, the captain more or less punched any question that I may have had out of my gut when he told me about the civilian crew manifest," replied the first officer.

"In that case, we wait until tomorrow. The Admiral told me that he needs 24 hours minimum before the Shiny Moon comes out of mothball," added the captain.

"What a liar. Knowing the dreck that constitutes the mothball maintenance personnel, that ship will need at least days, if not weeks, of cleaning, repair, and maintenance before she meets the minimum standard of combat worthiness."

"The Admiral told me that we are to do all of that once we are underway. Once the FTL engines come online, and the ship more or less keeps us alive in space, then we are to depart Sol for our mission."

"Must be some mission."

"You have no idea."

"Alright, in that case I'll head to the reserve fleet shipyards tomorrow and report in. How do civilians generally report and enlist for a ship?" asked Nicole.

"Depends. On the frontier, you just walk up to the guards and inquire if there are any slots open aboard. On Earth, you do the same, only we have to meet up for the first muster before embarking since the respective naval deployment has just started," replied the first officer.

"What he said, more or less. If the ship is ready, they will let you in, and you have to stand in a courtyard; if not, they will send you away. I would say midday tomorrow. Have the civilians report by then. FTL and life support, not to mention the reactor, do not take all that long to get online. Normally, it should be ready within an hour. What a disaster mothball has become," added the captain.

"What happens if we suffer a full-scale invasion from a rival power, say the Solar Empire?" asked Nicole as she got up and walked to the door; the two men did the same and followed.

"We lose," replied the first officer with all sincerity.

"The disadvantages of a republic; the heel upon your neck does not come from your own government; instead, it comes from the government that conquers yours," added the captain.

"Alright, sir, midday tomorrow we'll report, hopefully for muster. If not, we repeat the process daily until it is so. I recommend sending that message across the group chat."

"Good idea," replied the captain, who took out his personal computer and sent out: "Midday report for muster; if sent away, repeat daily until it is so."

The captain could hear the personal computer of his first officer beep and ring, indicating that the message had been sent and received. Thinking quickly, the captain realized that he should have worded it to be less casual; a single sentence sounded like a friend messaging his friends for a round of beer. He put it out of his mind quickly, however, when he realized that the crew, more or less, was not going to care. It has been ten years, after all, since they were subject to the disciplinary pressures of service.

"I'll see the both of you tomorrow, hopefully," said Nicole as she opened the door after putting on her shoes and walked out, still dressed in the captain's reserve uniform.

"Try to wear something else tomorrow," suggested the captain.

"Ah, we wouldn't want the sailors to confuse their commanding officer, now would we?" teased Nicole with a smile.

"The saddest part of that statement is the fact that it is more likely to be true than false," added the first officer.

"I'll message the pilot to descend and fly you to your respective apartments. First officer, see if you can get the old officer gang up and running again by tomorrow, and make sure that the sailors report daily. I understand that discipline was non-existent for a decade, but the republic has called us back to service, and discipline is what we will have until our deployment ends."

"I'll make sure of it, sir," replied the first officer.

"Excellent, and Nicole, make sure that your fellow working sisters report to the shipyards daily. The chances of us leaving tomorrow are high, but they are not guaranteed. If they are late, they miss their enlistment contract and chance to make enough money to retire."

"Trust me, with the amount of intrigue and wisdom that this specific occupation gives you, we'll be there 100%."

"Alright, I'll see the both of you soon. Dismissed," ordered the captain, and both Nicole and the first officer saluted; the first officer stood at attention and saluted perfectly, while Nicole remained as she was and saluted with an uneven arm and palm.

The two left the apartment, and the captain closed and locked the door behind them. He pulled out his personal computer yet again and messaged the pilot to land. He was to pick up the first officer and a new female passenger and deliver them to the respective destinations that they selected. Once that was done, the task for the Admiral would be completed, and the pilot would then be dismissed from his command. The pilot responded quickly, informing him that his orders had been received and understood.

Putting the personal computer back in his pocket, the captain walked back to his bedroom and took off his active-duty uniform. Once he did so, he hesitated for a moment, unsure if he should wear it again tomorrow. He decided against it; after all, he was about to call the Admiral and inform him of his progress in getting the crew back in order, and he planned to request some new threads. Folding the uniform away, he picked up a fresh, clean pair of reserve threads and put them on. He was much more comfortable now.

Lying down on the bed, he called the Admiralty Building, whose number he had saved as protocol. If during mothball something related to the potential readiness of his ship came up, he was to call this number and report the issue to admiralty command. He thought that whoever picked up on the other end would be able to, at the very least, get his message over to Admiral Hackett.

"Please report your dilemma," said a voice, feminine in tone, but a voice that Captain Nagy was unfamiliar with.

"I need to speak with Admiral Hackett. Is he busy?"

"Very busy. Who is this?"

"Very well, I need a message sent to him. This is William Nagy, Captain of the Cruiser-class vessel *Shiny Moon*."

After a slight pause and delay, the voice responded, "State your message."

"Procedures to reorient the crew towards active-duty status are progressing smoothly. The senior officers, myself included, have outgrown our old active-duty uniforms; I believe the same is true for the rest of the crew. Fresh uniforms should be provided as activation procedures are finalized. Furthermore, the civilian component has been obtained; however, the respective individuals who comprise said component are somewhat unorthodox. I trust that my full discretion to choose the civilians that I deem necessary also applies here. Finally, I recommend that the ship be ready for space by tomorrow noon; any longer, and ship effectiveness will take longer to establish up to minimum standard. That is all."

"Message received; I'll have it delivered to the Admiral," said the voice, and the woman on the other side of the line disconnected the call.

Exhausted and with nothing else to do but wait for tomorrow, the captain said, "Turn off all lights," and the apartment computer turned off the lights. The captain had all the windows of the apartment covered with several layers of tarp, and even though it was still the middle of the afternoon, the apartment was pitch black. The captain did not take long to fall asleep.

Chapter Five

The captain woke up to pitch-black darkness. He yelled out, "Turn on all lights," and the apartment was suddenly saturated with light. He checked the time; it was around 4 in the morning. He had slept for over twelve hours, plus some additional time. He felt strange; he could not put his mind to the cause of such a feeling until he realized what it was: his system was clear of alcohol.

He got up and walked around the apartment, wondering what to do. He had eight hours to go until noon, and passing time was not something that the captain was skilled at. He walked to the kitchen, prepared some breakfast, and ate it, all while looking at the news through his personal computer, which he held in his hand.

President Varis was announcing a new colonization project at the far end of the Perseus Arm in the Milky Way. Incredibly cheap real estate for anyone who was willing to lay claim to the different solar systems and begin human settlement. Organizations that could establish a 1,000-man colony were entitled to a single moon; 5,000, an entire planet; and 50,000 gave you the right to autonomously control an entire solar system, complete with local government.

"What a waste of human life," said the captain to himself.

Such colonization projects never end well. Rogue pirate elements raid the colonies, and rival civilizations scramble for the best systems by setting up colonies right next to the ones that the Republic of Earth establishes. Skirmishes break out, weak-willed politicians abandon entire systems in favor of others, and the lives and dreams of hundreds of thousands are extinguished.

Scrolling for more news stories, the captain found general judicial news: corruption scandal after corruption scandal. From the news that managed to reach the borders of the republic, there was the unfortunate news of crimes against humanity being committed in other rival human civilizations. The Solar Empire continued to defend the practice of slavery as necessary for the "continuation of a prosperous empire," citing the fact that the scientists who create the weapons should never have to fear the toil of labor.

Other nations were in a state of constant war, such as feudalistic nations, each solar system swearing allegiance to a king, with each system ruled by a duke, who assigned planets to counts and moons to barons. The free men who wished to live free, without a government to oppress them, did so by flying among the stars aboard massive vessels. They only stayed in a certain area for a limited amount of time; fellow free men who flew under the pirate flag and aggressive navies from large governments were always a concern.

"The Terraforming Installation," thought the captain, and he suddenly discovered what he was going to do for the next eight hours.

He left his personal computer on the sofa where he was seated and went to get the charging cable. He found it next to his bed on the nightstand, the same place where he had left it previously. Memory for Captain Nagy was a tricky thing, especially when events occurred with alcohol still in his veins.

Returning to the sofa, he located the nearby outlet, plugged in the charging cable, and then connected it to the end of the personal computer. Right before he took a seat, his eye caught sight of it. It was the vodka bottle from yesterday, around half full. Nicole had left it on the far corner of the kitchen counter, and Captain Nagy was astonished that he did not see it as he made breakfast. He blamed it on the personal computer that was distracting him as he prepared it.

He walked over to the bottle, the very bottle that he paid 100 credits for yesterday. He picked it up and felt the weight of the liquid; he could feel the power that the liquid contained as he held the bottle by its neck. Yet he was incredibly torn; his body was demanding that he pour a glass, but the last shreds of naval honor that remained alive after a decade of neglect kept reminding him of his duty.

His past flashed before his eyes. He saw the crew, his ship, the many missions, battles, tribulations, joys, and pains that they had all shared throughout their careers. The laughs, the sleepless weeks, the hours of fear when hunting enemy contacts across a solar system—he remembered it all. He missed those times, and he wanted to live them again.

Against all odds, the shreds of naval honor won. Captain Nagy opened the vodka bottle, walked over to the sink, and began to pour. The vodka splashed all around the sink, thanks to the height at which the captain was holding it. He could smell the strong odor of alcohol, and he could feel the tears his body was crying as the liquid it so desperately craved forever slipped from its grasp. He was mad with rage.

The bottle now empty, he turned around and threw it with as much force as he could muster against the wall. It smacked into the wall, shattering into many pieces and leaving behind several scratches on the wall paint. It was going to come out of his security deposit, but he could care less.

With the obstacle that was in his way now surpassed, the captain returned to the sofa and took a seat. Grabbing his personal computer, he searched the internet of Earth for every piece of information he could find regarding the Terraforming Installation. The myth and legend that he spent a career mocking, he now treated with the utmost respect and interest.

He decided to look at the beginning, all the way back to its supposed creation. It was the greatest achievement of the Human Unity, the civilization that existed in the early days when all of mankind stood together under a single flag. It was a republic, run in much the same way as the Republic of Earth is run. All human differences united under a single government.

The Terraforming Installation was supposed to be the first of many. Its existence was never confirmed by the Human Unity or the Republic of Earth, the nation that more or less inherited the vast majority of her classified archives and databases. It was the culmination of the best minds across humanity: a fully sentient and fully autonomous massive space installation that could terraform any world into paradise.

No matter the orbit, it could drag the respective world into the star's Goldilocks zone. No matter the harshness of the climate, it could be transformed into paradise. Random planetoids? They could be turned into moons to help with the tides. Even the gravity itself, with careful manipulation of the core and the introduction or removal of super-heavy elements, could be modified. The DNA and gametes of trillions of organisms, some from creatures that originated on Earth and others created by the artificial intelligence that operates the Terraforming Installation, were all stored and ready to be seeded on new worlds.

The AI was the hallmark of the AI development team, which existed during the glory days of the Human Unity. Based on a human neural matrix, the AI was designed to be self-aware, resilient to damage, and able to adapt and improve upon not just itself but the Terraforming Installation that served as its body. It was to choose the best worlds to terraform initially, and once trials were over, it was to begin the terraforming of every possible planet and moon in the galaxy.

Everything else that was available was more legend than fact. Even the above was part of the myth; no one ever confirmed the existence of the AI development team or the construction of the Terraforming Installation. No human civilization, as of today, has managed to develop fully sentient AI, and the terraforming technologies that are available only work for worlds that already exist in the habitable zone of a respective star. Even then, the process takes centuries to begin and complete.

Captain Nagy closed the internet browser on his personal computer and checked the time. He had only burned a quarter of an hour! Sighing as he resigned himself to his fate, he opened the internet browser yet again and began to browse every single technical manual related to Republic of Earth cruisers that he could find.

It was eleven in the morning, and the captain was just about ready to crush the personal computer in his hand when the preset alarm he had set went off. At long last, eleven in the morning had finally arrived! Captain Nagy was all set; his reserve uniform was up to code, and he walked to the apartment door and turned around.

He saw his small, humble apartment, an apartment that was affordable enough on his reservist salary. He was not going to miss it one bit. Captain Nagy opened the door, walked outside the apartment, and turned around to lock the door behind him. If lucky, he would never have to see this apartment again.

Without the naval pilot to act as a chauffeur, Captain Nagy would have to walk to the mothball shipyard on foot. He wasted no time, heading down the staircase of his apartment for the last time before opening the apartment complex door and stepping outside onto the sidewalk. He turned left and began to walk.

Directions to the mothball shipyard were not that difficult; it was directly ahead for approximately three miles. Captain Nagy walked at a normal pace, and in forty-five minutes, he arrived at the shipyard.

He was glad to see that a great crowd of reservist sailors was already gathered around the main gate. Yet he was ecstatic when he saw the Shiny Moon, nose up to the sky, resting on one of the launch pads.

"Captain Nagy, sir!" yelled one of the reservist sailors as soon as he identified his old captain's face. The crowd erupted in applause and cheer, and they greeted him with handshakes and pats on the back as he approached everyone.

"After a decade, we are back!" yelled Captain Nagy so that his sailors could hear. They sang space shanties and cheers; a few sailors snuck in a drink from a flask.

"Indeed, we are back at long last," said the first officer of the Shiny Moon, who was leaning on the brick wall that separated the mothball shipyard from the rest of the city.

"How's my crew doing?" asked the captain, who walked over to his first officer and extended his arm for a handshake, which was reciprocated.

"Drunk, tired from lack of sleep, and all around doing terribly from sitting on their rears for the last ten years. Other than that, they are the same men we served with a decade ago. I think they can come back with some gentle care and discipline."

"I'm glad to hear it. And the civilians? I don't see any of the women who are supposed to be our civilian crew component in this crowd."

"They all arrived a half-hour early from the noon deadline. The guards let them in; I reckon it is for processing and likely to see how the hell the navy is going to get away with enlisting a thousand prostitutes for service," replied the first officer, whose smile betrayed just how funny the situation was to him.

"Admiral Hackett said to form a crew; I formed a crew. The navy can't complain when I follow orders."

"Either way, I'm happy to be back among the stars. Every single sailor here knows that up there is our home."

"I agree with every word," replied the captain, and the conversation died down.

The sailors of the Shiny Moon waited for another hour until the guards opened the gates and informed everyone that they were allowed to enter. They were to follow a group of sentinel guards to the muster field and await a briefing from their captain.

The sailors poured through the gate. The captain and the first officer waited in the back for the sailors to enter before heading in. One of the guards immediately identified the captain and walked up to him with a small letter envelope in hand.

"From Admiral Hackett, sir. He wants you to read it before addressing your men in the muster speech," relayed the guard, holding out the letter.

"Thank you," replied the captain, taking the envelope from the guard.

The captain opened the envelope and took out a folded sheet of paper. It was standard non-classified type, usually used by the Admiralty to flex power by having their communications hand-delivered. It also served as a great way to send messages that would be embarrassing if the message were intercepted before the recipient received it.

Captain Nagy unfolded the sheet of paper and began to read.

"*Captain William Nagy, you are one crazy son of a bitch. I wish you could see the face of the Commodore whom you met yesterday as he raced into my office. He informed me that a certain Captain in my chain of command thought it best to enlist over a thousand sex workers as the effective entirety of his civilian personnel. The entire city is hearing about it, and my office is getting calls from every single admiral in the Republic; even the Secretary of Defense took some time out of his schedule to speak with me regarding this most intriguing incident!*"

"*I don't know who you spoke to, but you have several politicians who are gunning for you. Their assistants arrived at my office late last night, expressing the desire of their bosses to see this 'project' unfold. This makes my job much easier; I, after all, did authorize you to choose the crew that you need in order to complete this mission. As such, I wish you good fortune and a skillful hand in managing your crew. Considering the composition of said crew, I have a feeling that you will need both.*"

"*Finally, as a reward for your iron-heavy balls, I made sure that a bottle of that fine bourbon which you enjoyed in my office made its way into the safe in your captain's quarters, alongside a few glasses. I am sure that it will come in handy during your mission, alongside the dossier that is next to it. With regards, Hackett.*"

Captain Nagy smiled at the positive news from the Admiral, folded the sheet of paper back into a small rectangle, and placed it back into the envelope before putting the envelope into his reserve uniform shirt pocket. He turned to his first officer before speaking.

"Let's go and brief the crew," said the captain to his first officer as he started to walk towards the muster field.

"It has been a long time since I heard those words; it is good to hear them again," replied the first officer as he followed the captain to the muster field.

"Indeed, first officer; indeed."

The men were already lined up in formation and ready to hear their muster speech, a speech that many among the crowd had waited over ten years to hear. The captain walked up to the elevated stage, stood behind the podium, adjusted the microphone so that it was level with his mouth, and then started to speak.

"For ten years, a miserable decade, we have lived in misery and squalor. We were fortunate; we had a reservist salary to keep us afloat, enough for a meager apartment, meager food, and a small portion for the vices that have stimulated our lives as best they could. I'm a shell of what I once was, and I can clearly see among the faces of my crew that we are all mere shells of the sailors that we once were."

"We've been in a battle for over ten years, and we've come out alive. I do not fault a single sailor here for the vices and decisions that you have made over the last ten years; I would be the greatest hypocrite on Earth if I were to do so. And I do not expect 100% out of you today; I'll save that for tomorrow!"

"I want you to look up there." Captain Nagy turned and pointed to the Shiny Moon sitting on a launchpad. "Look at our old ship. We can see that her paint has faded, and we know that she has been left to squalor, the same as us! But she is still kicking, she can still fly, and I can bet that she has the guts to make it off the surface of this planet! Our old bird is still intact, the same as us!"

"Our mission is not going to be easy, but there is a reason for our activation. I can assure you that the mission is of great importance to the Republic, important enough that the Shiny Moon may end up living in the public consciousness! What an honor for the old bird to be given one last chance at glory, after all that she has been through, after all that her crew has been through!" The sailors cheered slightly.

"Dammit already, we are breaking discipline and protocol, and we are not even aboard ship! But what the hell, have you seen our civilian crew roster lately?" asked the captain, and the crew yelled and cheered strongly.

"Report to stations, make sure that the idiot engineers in the mothball shipyard did not make a mess of my ship, and may glory find us all! Dismissed!" concluded the captain, and the crew cheered as they peeled off like a swarm of ants, racing to board the ship that they had been denied access to for so long.

The captain leaned on the podium and smiled as the first officer climbed the stage and joined him.

"A good speech, sir."

"Thank you, first officer; it was rusty, but rust is all we have for now until we rub it out of our systems. Now we wait for the civilian crew to report to their muster."

"I'm looking forward to it," said the first officer with a large grin as he walked away and stepped off the stage.

The captain waited for ten or so minutes until the crowd of civilians began to exit a nearby building and report to the muster field. They were all, with the exception of a few men, dressed in regular women's clothes and coats, and they arrived as a single group and stood still and at attention, just like the sailor crowd before them. The captain was impressed; this was the best civilian muster that he had ever seen throughout his career of command.

"Civilians, it is an honor and privilege to give this muster to you. It is obvious and apparent that you are breaking many norms and protocols here today; 95% of you, after all, are women, and women who come from unique occupations. Some may say that such difference is a liability; I, however, and I speak with decades of experience when I say this, see you as a tremendous asset. Today, we stand on sacred soil, the soil of Earth, the birthplace of our species."

"This soil has carried mankind for hundreds of thousands of years. It has nurtured us when we first evolved, it has nurtured us as we spread out across the planet, and it has provided the initial food and seeds that we needed in order to seed life on other worlds. While there are tens of thousands of worlds like Earth out there, none of them would be so if this humble little world did not come first."

"What was the common truth throughout this history? The one who is unique, who sees with a different perspective, gifts us all. The inventor, the dreamer, the one who says that this world is not all that there is; it is thanks to them that we are where we are today. I welcome each and every one of you. You are hardworking; you have dealt with decades of insults and obstacles, and you are still here, fighting and kicking. I need civilians with guts on my crew roster, civilians who will not lay down and quit when the universe kicks them down. I am happy to see that I not only have such a civilian crew, but I also have the best civilian crew in the fleet!"

"Do your duties well, use your unique skills to the fullest, stuff your wallets and your purses with all the credits that you can spare, and serve your Republic with honor and pride! Dismissed!" finished the captain, and the civilian crew began to peel off like a swarm of ants, racing toward the ship.

There, however, remained one individual among the crowd who did not race toward the ship; she waited until she was alone before walking toward the stage.

Chapter Six

"Well, look at this," remarked the first officer as she approached the stage.

"I had a feeling that they would choose you as the civilian liaison," added the captain as a fully uniformed Nicole climbed the stage to join the two other officers.

"The crew overwhelmingly voted for me once the decision came up, sir."

"Well, I'm proud to have you aboard, ensign. Report to your station," ordered the captain.

"Right away, sir," replied Nicole, and she stepped off the platform after a brief salute and went off in the direction of the Shiny Moon.

"Interesting dilemma, sir," said the first officer.

"Oh?" asked the captain.

"Not only is she breaking protocol when she sleeps with you, but she is also breaking protocol when she sleeps with any other sailor who is not an ensign. So many intriguing possibilities as to how this can go."

"It's quite simple: this entire crew will likely accumulate hundreds of thousands of protocol violations, and I just pardon them all once the mission is over. Simple and easy," said the captain as he stepped off the stage and started to walk toward his ship.

"The move of a bastard, a move that I agree with 100%," added the first officer, who stepped off the stage and joined his commanding officer.

The two men walked slowly to the ship in order to save themselves from having to queue up for the ship elevators. When in the upright launch position, or when a ship generates gravity through torch propulsion, the compartments rotate in blocks that lock to the elevator shafts. As such, the only way up or down on a planetary surface is through the elevators, which get very congested when over two thousand crew members decide to board all at once. Even when packed into each elevator like sardines, ship boarding is a process that takes some time.

The captain and the first officer arrived at the launch pad, and as they suspected, the crowd was still heavy with crew members who were awaiting their turn to board an elevator. The captain and first officer decided to wait at the base of the launch pad staircase and check periodically to see if the crowd had dissipated.

"Cleared for FTL travel in under 24 hours—I know that mothballed ships need to be maintained periodically, but after 10 years, apparently our bird is as good as new? I have an uneasy feeling about this," remarked the first officer to start the small talk.

"Look at it this way: if we all blow up in mid-launch, we at least get to die sailors. Better that than dying face-first on your bar counter," replied the captain with a smile.

"I swear that you were my most regular patron, and no one ever knew that you were a captain. Much less my captain."

"Why would they? Not a single sailor from our ship showed up, and your patrons were regular working types for the most part, who just want to unwind after a day's work."

"I blame the brothel bars. You get girls and alcohol; it costs much more than patronizing my bar, but I could never compete with that."

"Well, hopefully your nephew manages to keep the place open. I would not want The Shiny Moon bar to go out of business; it's the only nice place in that miserable street block. Speaking of your nephew, you never talk about your brother. Is there a reason?"

"My brother ran off to the frontier and left his son behind. His wife was a demon, so I can't blame him completely, but I'm still bitter about it to this day. He left all his Earth possessions and money behind for his son, at least."

"I see. Do you speak often?"

"He stopped messaging me some six years ago. Knowing how much he likes to talk and keep in touch, I reckon that he is dead. Probably a raid from either pirates or one of the other human civilizations out there in the frontier."

"I see. I apologize for bringing it up."

"No need, sir. We all die someday; he at least died free."

"I'll go check the crowd," the captain said as he walked up the staircase to the launch pad.

A few moments passed, and the captain walked back down.

"Nope, still a few people. Much less than before, however. A few more minutes and we can head up."

"Alright, you choose the topic, sir."

The captain was about to speak until he realized that the first officer was not informed about the nature of the mission. He decided that it would be best for him to be informed alongside the rest of the officers during their first mission meeting. He picked another topic of conversation to discuss.

"Since credits are useless while onboard, how often are you going to visit our civilian crew?" asked the captain with a smile.

"Often, sir. You?"

"Often. We are all going to be broke after this mission."

"Why do you think your newest civilian liaison had such an easy time convincing them to sign up for service?" added the first officer with a laugh.

"At least we get to charitably fund the retirement of a thousand civilians; much better use of our tax dollars than throwing it into the disaster that we call our nation's military service pension fund," replied the captain with a smile.

"Alright, I think we killed all the small talk that was in us today. Let us go up to the launch pad and wait a few more minutes until an empty elevator to the bridge appears," suggested the first officer.

"You are right, as always," replied the captain, and the two men climbed the staircase leading up to the launch pad and joined the small crowd of sailors and civilian personnel, who saluted and then rested at ease as the two men arrived.

It took several more minutes, but eventually, the elevators started to come back empty. The captain and the first officer boarded one and pressed the button leading to the bridge. The elevator went up, and in a few moments, they were back home.

It was a decently sized bridge, with around two dozen seats all around the different consoles at the sides, and the captain's chair at the center. The first officer sat in a chair to the right of the captain's chair, while the ship's bosun sat in a chair to the left of the captain's chair. The captain's chair, the first officer's chair, and the bosun's chair all had consoles in front, with different displays, buttons, and toggle switches, all corresponding to their respective roles.

Finally, the helmsman and the navigation team sat in front of the captain, the first officer, and the bosun. They were near the front of the bridge, allowing the captain, in his unique position, to obtain more or less an eagle-eyed view of the bridge. Furthermore, the only chair that could swivel aboard the bridge was the captain's chair, fitting for his task as observer over the bridge.

The captain and the first officer walked over to their respective chairs and took a seat. The captain was pleased; the mothball technicians never bothered to change the old cushioning, and the seat more or less folded into submission as soon as its old master took a seat.

The captain, however, felt that there was something missing, and he realized it immediately when he looked down and remembered that he was still in his reserve uniform.

"First officer, I have a small favor to ask of you," the captain said.

"Name it, sir," replied the first officer.

"Remind the bosun to signal a change of clothing into active-duty dress as soon as we are underway."

"It will be done, sir."

Wanting to get accustomed to his old crew once again, Captain Nagy began to swivel and observe his bridge. The bosun, helmsman, and first officer were the same—a welcome sign. The respective sensor, gunnery, and engineering officers, on the other hand, while mostly the same faces, had a few differences.

"What happened to Lieutenant Junior Grade Ramirez?" asked the captain, looking at the gunnery suite of the bridge.

"Dead from liver cirrhosis, sir," replied one of the gunnery officers.

"How long ago?"

"Three years, sir."

"What about Ensign Hakalski?" asked the captain, looking at the sensor suite of the bridge.

"Fight with some street ruffians; he died after a week in the hospital. The bastards were executed a few months after that, thankfully," replied one of the sensor officers.

"How long ago?"

"Seven years, sir."

"Bosun, do you have access to the present sailor manifest?" asked the captain.

"Yes, sir," replied the bosun, who immediately flicked through some of his screens until it came up.

"How much of my original crew is present aboard my ship?"

The bosun took around a minute to tally up the respective data and results and calculate a rough estimate: "Around 73%, sir."

"Almost 30% casualties, stupid politicians killed my men!" roared the captain to himself.

"Thank you, bosun. Carry on."

"Yes, sir."

The captain swiveled around, staring intently at the new faces on his bridge. They were junior faces, no doubt fresh graduates waiting for their first assignment. They worked their consoles perfectly under protocol; they still did not know the respective shortcuts of efficiency—the ones that only come from years on the job.

"First officer, I'll be in my quarters. You have the bridge."

"Understood, sir."

The captain got up from his chair and walked toward his quarters. The door opened automatically once it detected his presence and closed behind him as the captain entered. The small room was just as he remembered. In one corner stood a desk with a small chair next to it. Next to the desk was a safe where classified documents and other valuables were kept. Hanging from the safe handle was a uniform wrapped in plastic. On the opposite side, there was a foldable bed frame that tucked into the wall when not in use.

The captain walked over to the plastic-wrapped uniform and took it out of the covering. Full active-duty dress, with the heavy decorations and shine that only a captain's uniform has. Captain Nagy undressed and put on his active-duty uniform. It fit perfectly. He was surprised at the fit, especially since he had not been measured before boarding the ship. More likely than not, the navy used the latest measurements and weight data from his most recent medical physical.

The captain, now properly dressed, opened his safe; the old combination that he still remembered from a decade ago still worked. Inside, he found the dossier that he had read in Admiral Hackett's office, alongside a corked bottle of fine bourbon with a few glasses tied around it. Smiling at the generous gift from the Admiral, Captain Nagy pulled out the dossier and flicked through it once again before returning it to the safe. He would bring it with him once he addressed the officers during their first mission meeting.

Properly dressed as a captain, Captain Nagy left his quarters, the door opening and closing automatically as he did so. The bridge crew, with the exception of the new faces who jumped up immediately, did not flinch nor make any attempt to deviate from their current task.

"CAPTAIN ON THE BRIDGE!" yelled one of the new faces, startled by the lack of protocol displayed by the sailors, as loudly as he could.

"Thank you, Ensign," replied Captain Nagy with a smile as he took a seat in his chair.

"There is no need, Ensign. The captain prefers that we remain focused on our duties instead of breaking them to show respect. Still, your attention to protocol has been noted," added the first officer.

"I see; thank you, sir," replied the ensign as he returned to his console.

"I see that the uniform fits you well, Captain," quipped the first officer.

"It is much better than the previous one."

"You looked like a mummy wrapped in naval thread in that dress."

"And you looked like a mummy who did not let himself go, First Officer."

"Someone had to remain combat-worthy among this crew."

"Sitting in a chair does not require strength, my First Officer."

"But command does."

"Alright, you've won that argument," admitted the captain.

A few minutes passed aboard the ship, and the captain was beginning to grow impatient with the preparations for launch. He decided to get some answers from the only man who could give them.

"Bosun, do you have a line to engineering?"

"Yes, sir."

"Open a line."

The bosun, in mere moments, opened a line to engineering. "Yes, bridge?" asked the head engineer.

"This is Captain William Nagy; first and foremost, how have you been, you old bastard!"

"Good, sir. I missed your perfect blend of charm and, well, nagging."

"Nagging? What do you mean, engineer?"

"It comes with the name: Nagy, he who nags."

"I see. Well, how's my old girl?"

"She's kicking, with pneumonia," replied the head engineer angrily.

"Let me guess, mothball technicians neglected her."

"You could say that."

"How badly?" asked the captain directly.

"The electrical grid is shot; they never replaced it. Hell, they never bothered to even clean it. The boys have found some faint dust and some rat droppings so far; the entire grid is more or less how it was a decade ago."

"When you say shot, what do I not have?"

"No lasers, for one. The power we need to run from the reactor to the turrets will burst the cables; that I can more or less guarantee you. That is all I can tell you right now; the other bad news we're still discovering."

"Thanks, engineering. Bosun, cut the line," hissed the captain in anger.

"Cut, sir."

"Well, there goes a third of our armament, assuming the railgun turrets and missile launchers are operational," added the first officer.

"Ripping out the cabling and replacing it with a fresh batch will take months. As much as I want to do it, we cannot for this mission. Rails and missiles will allow us to more or less take on a destroyer or frigate; anything else and our shields and armor will fail before theirs do," added the captain.

"I'm assuming that hostilities are a strong possibility, captain?"

"They are indeed, first officer."

"Well then, we are going to have to learn how to run away."

"The only bastards who should be running away are the politicians; once we flick a match inside their rat nest and set it ablaze!"

For another half hour, the crew labored tirelessly to get the Shiny Moon to launch-ready status. Life support was online more or less immediately after the crew started to board; the sub-light torch engines and FTL warper engines, however, took some additional time.

"Well, engineering?" asked an impatient captain.

"You have a 79% chance of operational FTL warper engines and a 94% chance of operational sub-light torch engines," replied the engineer.

"How much longer until you can push up the percentages to 99% across the board?"

"That would take us days, sir."

"Very well, bosun, sound liftoff stations."

"Yes, sir. *Attention all hands, please man your liftoff stations. Attention all hands, please man your liftoff stations,*" said the bosun, his orders echoing by loudspeaker all across the ship.

The bosun's call to stations roared across the loudspeakers scattered throughout the Shiny Moon. The faint vibration of sound traveling through the bulkheads added a bass-like effect to the loudspeaker that blasted the call to the bridge. It was a majestic little system that worked like a charm even after a decade of complete and utter abandonment.

"Bosun, open a line to all ship departments."

"Open, sir," replied the bosun after a few moments.

"Engineering, status?"

"Green, Captain."

"Sensor suite, status?"

"Green, Captain."

"Gunnery suite, status?"

"Green, Captain."

"All departments ready, Captain," added the bosun.

"Perfect, let us rock and roll then. Keep the lines to all departments open, bosun, as per standard liftoff regulation."

"Yes, sir."

Chapter Seven

"Helm, status?" asked the captain.

"Ready to begin. T-minus 10 on your order," replied the helmsman.

"Bosun, open a line to shipyard central departure."

"Yes, Shiny Moon?" asked the shipyard departure controller.

"We are ready to launch, awaiting your confirmation and permission."

"We confirm your readiness; permission granted, Shiny Moon."

"Helmsman, begin," ordered the captain.

"T-minus 10, 9, 8, 7, 6, 5, 4, 3, 2, 1. Launch!"

One could feel a slight kick as the chemical rockets attached to the sides of the ship activated all at once. The kick was slight, and it took several seconds before the Shiny Moon generated enough lift with the chemical rockets alone to start gaining altitude. The captain was not pleased.

"Engineering, the moment we start to drop altitude, screw regulation and use just enough torch drive to get us into orbit."

"Yes, captain; however, we must wait until we reach an altitude of at least 5,000 ft. Any lower, and minimal torch drive risks destroying a decent chunk of the shipyard city."

"Of course; may the chemical rockets keep us alive until then."

The Shiny Moon continued to gain altitude, albeit very slowly due to its immense mass. This was one of the most dangerous moments for any ship that has to lift off from a densely populated area. No matter the tens of thousands of complaints filed by captains and admirals across the fleet, the Secretary of the Navy and the rest of the executive government continued to uphold the practice of storing mothballed vessels on the surface.

Easier to maintain and easier to justify keeping them mothballed, but terrible for the ships themselves, the crew currently manning the ship, and the unfortunate souls who must, out of economic necessity, live near the mothball shipyards. A complete and utter travesty, all thanks to the ingenious mothball proposal by Senator Jonathan Varis.

The Shiny Moon started to slowly increase in velocity, climbing up the different levels of the atmosphere a few minutes at a time. The chemical rockets ended up working this time, but one cannot say the same for the few incidents where a launch had catastrophic results on the world that the ship was mothballed at.

"Captain, we've reached the exosphere," relayed the helmsman.

"Excellent. Helmsman, begin to assist our chemical rockets with 0.1% torch engine capacity."

"Yes, captain."

The torch engines turned on, and even at the smallest possible thrust they could produce, they doubled the total thrust output of the ship. The rockets were more or less useless at this point.

"Helm, can we ditch the useless mass that is attached all around our ship? They are obsolete after just 0.1% of torch engine capacity."

"Certainly, captain; programming them to return to Earth."

The chemical rockets detached and rocketed off in the opposite direction, returning to Earth. They are reusable and will no doubt be used again in another launch. The captain wasted no time.

"Bosun, sound general stations. Helm, prepare for regular departure drive once the compartments rotate into place."

"Right away, captain!"

"Understood, sir."

In a simultaneous motion, the glaring yell of the loudspeaker merged with the activation of the gravity deck plates, the inertial stabilizers, and the inertial dampeners, followed finally by the rotation of the compartments. The feeling was similar to that of a rollercoaster dropping from the highest peak, combined with the sensation of a swaying boat on the sea. The sensation lasted for around a minute until the deck compartments rotated into place and the gravity and inertia systems activated fully.

"Helm, 10% torch engine capacity, followed by 25% when we are sufficiently away from Earth. Set course for the nearest Lagrange point."

"Yes, captain."

"Engineering, prepare the FTL warper engines for activation."

"Right away, Captain."

No kick of any kind was felt by the crew of the *Shiny Moon*. Even with the great g-force that 10% torch engine capacity inflicts upon the ship, the advanced system of gravity generators, inertial stabilizers, and inertial dampeners prevents anything other than a stable 1g downward force from affecting both the ship and her crew. Without these three vital systems, space travel would be much less pleasant.

The ship traveled along for a few minutes until it was at a sufficiently far distance from Earth to allow for the increase of the torch engine capacity to 25%. This allowed the *Shiny Moon* to accelerate greatly, reaching the Lagrange point in just under fifteen minutes. The ship slowed down to a standstill and was now ready to enter FTL.

"Alright. Helm, prepare initial FTL heading; aim for the border between the Republic of Earth and Solar Empire space," ordered the Captain.

"Yes, Captain."

"Bosun, open a line to engineering."

"Open, Captain."

"Engineering, do we have FTL?"

"Yes, Captain, but I'd go slow, 2.00c-3.00c before we crank up the warpers any higher."

"Just two to three times the speed of light?"

"Yes, Captain. I do not feel comfortable going any faster until I see them in operation for at least a few hours."

"Very well, prepare the warpers for 2.00c, then increase to 3.00c when you feel comfortable enough to do so, Engineer. Helmsman, match that speed as soon as engineering gives you an all-clear."

"Yes, Captain."

"Yes, Captain."

"Bosun, cut the line to engineering and open a line to medical."

The bosun did as the Captain ordered, and in a few moments, the line to medical was opened. The head doctor was the one to answer.

"Yes, bridge?"

"How's the health of my crew? Do note that they suffered a severe famine of the spirit for over a decade."

"The good news is everything that ails your crew, I can fix. The bad news is that I and the medical staff are not going to get much sleep for weeks."

"I see. What ails them?"

"Liver cirrhosis from excessive drinking and an infestation of venereal diseases. The liver issues we can treat with stem cell implantation and the removal of scarred tissue. Plenty of surgeries, but the crew will live. The venereal diseases, for the most part, can be treated with a cocktail of antibiotic and antiviral injections. I would strongly suggest that the sailors and civilian crew refrain from seeing each other intimately for at least a few days. It would make our jobs in medical much easier."

"Of course. Bosun, write and then send a general communication over personal computer; the regulation forbidding sexual relations aboard ship will remain in place for a full week in order to eradicate all venereal disease aboard ship."

"I'll get on it right away, sir," replied the bosun.

"Thank you, Captain," replied the head doctor.

"Of course, Doctor. Finally, how is the mental health of my crew?"

"Not good, but I believe everyone will be back to their old selves in a few weeks. We will keep an extensive eye on everyone and keep you apprised if any trends, whether good or bad, develop."

"Perfect, in that case, carry on, Doctor. Bosun, cut the line."

"Cut, sir."

"Bosun, send a priority message to the head officers. In two hours, I want to have an officers' meeting. Assuming the mothball technicians did not remove it for whatever reason, it will take place in the briefing room."

"Right away, Captain," replied the bosun, who got to work.

"First officer, leave my bridge and get dressed in your active-duty uniform. Return once dressed."

"Yes, sir," replied the first officer with a smile as he got up and left.

"Feels good to be back, doesn't it, sir?" asked the bosun with a smile.

"Damn straight, sailor. Now get back to work on sending that message."

"Yes, sir."

Two uneventful hours had passed. No problems arose, and the ship entered FTL a quarter hour after it had stopped to a standstill at the Lagrange point. The Captain inquired about the delay, which turned out to be an overprecaution by the engineering team. The delay was granted, and the *Shiny Moon* traveled the cosmos at a comfortable 3.00c, or three times the speed of light.

"Bosun, you have the bridge until the first officer and I return," ordered the Captain, who was holding the dossier given to him by Admiral Hackett in his hand.

"Yes, Captain," replied the bosun, and the two men left the bridge.

"I'm surprised that the ship is running smoothly so far," said the first officer as the two men entered an elevator and selected the deck where the briefing room was located.

"We are traveling at just 3.00c; I don't think we even left the Sol system yet," replied the Captain with a snarl.

"Overprecaution is better than carelessness."

"Of course, first officer; but traveling at 3.00c is an insult to the ship."

"I can't argue with that," admitted the first officer.

The men remained silent as the elevator descended to the appropriate deck. They got out and walked to the briefing room, where the officers' meeting was to take place. The room, when they arrived, was filled with officers, the majority of whom were still in their reserve uniforms. As soon as the Captain and first officer walked in, everyone got up, stood at attention, and saluted.

"At ease, everyone," said the Captain, and everyone sat back down.

"Alright, we are going to get right to it." The Captain opened up the dossier and dropped it on the meeting table. "First and foremost, what does everyone here know about the Terraforming Installation?"

"That's the mission!" blurted out the head gunnery officer in astonishment.

"Yes, orders straight from the mouth of Admiral Hackett."

"Alright, tell us everything that is in that dossier, sir," asked the head sensor officer.

"The dossier, first and foremost, is a recovered and translated Solar Empire dossier. They have discovered several worlds that, for all intents and purposes, are literally carbon copies of Earth, especially the carbon-based lifeforms that have been detected on said worlds. There are several, and each and every one is the first world to harbor complex ecosystem life that humanity has discovered in the galaxy."

"How the hell did we get a hold of this?" asked the head engineer.

"Clandestine Intelligence got a hold of it."

"Seriously? They, out of all people, managed to obtain it?" added the head gunnery officer.

"That's exactly what Admiral Hackett said."

"Oh, I see what he's doing," the head gunnery officer said with a smile.

"Please, do elaborate, officer."

"He wants to start a war so that his fleet gets out of mothball."

"Has the fool gone mad?" asked the head sensor officer.

The head gunnery officer was taken aback at the question, and it took a few moments before he responded to the head sensor officer.

"No, he has not."

"I get that he wants the fleet out of mothball, but instigating a conflict, assuming that is the purpose of this mission, is something that simply crosses every line that we have been taught not to cross."

"Gentlemen, if we may return to the briefing."

"Sorry, sir," replied the head sensor officer.

"You are right, head gunnery officer; I have no doubt in my mind that the Admiral wants a war. He is tired of sitting on his ass all day and rotting away, seeing his sailors die of misery and decline, all because our current President wants to save a few credits for wholly inefficient bureaucratic programs. Frankly, I do not think there is a single man or woman in this room who is against what the Admiral is trying to do, especially when you consider the fact that this dossier strongly supports the existence of the Terraforming Installation. Imagine each and every planet and moon in our entire galaxy, fully terraformed and able to support life. It would be paradise. It certainly beats drinking myself to death."

"Damn right, sir," replied the head gunnery officer.

"This is the plan. We are going to take this rust bucket, and we are going to verify these coordinates. If the Earth-like planets really exist, then we send out a message. But that is not all. You have my permission to submit a request for court martial to the Admiralty; you even have my permission to remove me from my command, but not before I ask one favor from all of you. If those

Imperial bastards from the Solar Empire have their paws all over these planets, then we are including the fact that we discovered the Terraforming Installation in Solar Empire space in our message."

"The Admirals and Generals will no doubt orchestrate a false flag operation if we do that," added the head gunnery officer with a smile, who immediately understood what the captain meant to do in such a situation.

"Dammit, sir, have you gone insane as well?" asked the head sensor officer in frustration.

"Like I said, once it is done, remove me from command and request a court martial."

"Dammit, you fool, can't you see it? Our Republic is dying, the military has gotten soft, our ships are more rust than iron. We need this war!" retorted the head gunnery officer.

"What about the billions that would die?" yelled the head sensor officer.

"What about the trillions who will live lives of paradise on terraformed worlds? Your soft spine grew up on Earth; I enlisted as a young man from the frontier. Having to breathe stale air inside your habitation dome, never being able to go outside without a suit, dying in your forties from cancer thanks to the high radiation from no atmosphere—what about them?" yelled the head gunnery officer.

"Captain, this is wrong," added the head engineer.

"It is, my old friend, but the captain is right," replied the first officer.

The briefing room quickly descended into anarchy, with the pro-war and anti-war sides quickly forming and arguing. The captain tried multiple times to gain command of the room, but he failed each and every time. The arguing was on the verge of morphing into violence until an incredibly loud and high-pitched sound silenced the room into submission.

"Gahhh! What was that?" shrieked the head gunnery officer.

"A little whistle that I decided to bring on board as a memento; never thought that I would have to use it aboard an apparently civilized military vessel," replied Ensign Nicole, the civilian liaison.

"Why the hell would you ever need such a thing?" asked the head gunnery officer, who, like everyone else in the room except Nicole, was suffering from sharp pain in their ears.

"It comes in useful when a client decides not to listen to instruction; now that I think about it, it comes in useful in any situation where a man does not listen."

"Well, Ensign, you have whatever is left of our hearing; speak your mind," said the captain, his ears still ringing from the sound.

"Thank you, sir. I want to remind everyone here that there is a particular fact that you have not mentioned so far. The Solar Empire has a slavery economy, where the slaves perform all of the labor, while the military and scientific classes enjoy lives of military service and scientific thought."

"They discovered all of these planets by themselves, and considering that we are still quite far from arriving at the border, and then clandestinely slipping in before we arrive at these planets—I assume, of course, since the captain has not gotten to their location so far in the briefing—there is no doubt that they will have the planets colonized and claimed before we even arrive."

"Furthermore, they likely know much more about this Terraforming Installation than we do. From what I have heard over the years from many different sailors, this station is supposedly self-aware and can create another Earth whenever it wants. Imagine how easily the Solar Empire will destroy us if every single world that they have is like Earth, while the vast majority of our worlds still lack atmosphere."

"Don't be like the rest of your gender. I've seen and been with thousands of men; the vast majority of them are completely and utterly useless. A few, on the other hand, turn out to be quite good. Be the good, not the bad. There are too many bad versions of you screwing up the galaxy already; we don't need more of them," finished Ensign Nicole.

"Fine, you damn fools. It is your conscience and legacy; I won't oppose your efforts," conceded the head sensor officer.

"I'll take all the blame for it. Your entries in the history books will remain clean, I can assure you. I wired the rogue missile that started the war, after all," said the head gunnery officer, and everyone in the room laughed at his jest.

Chapter Eight

The meeting continued undisturbed for three entire hours until the captain concluded it. With more or less universal support among the officers, and the few who disagreed pledging not to stand in the way, the conspiracy to ensure that the war Admiral Hackett wants becomes a reality was born.

For the next few months, the Shiny Moon slowly picked up her FTL speed once the head engineer felt confident in the health and integrity of the FTL warpers. The ship arrived at the border between the Republic of Earth and the Solar Empire. The first system that supposedly harbors a fully terraformed Earth was located in Imperial space close to the border, near the edge of a small nebula, which Terran survey analysis had time and again confirmed to be useless space for any sort of potential colonization.

"Captain, entering their space is a serious provocation," said the bosun, who could not help reminding the captain of this truth.

"Indeed, bosun. I must remind you that our objective is located in their space. Helmsman, take us in, and try to avoid detection. The bosun gave a good reason why we should avoid it as much as possible."

"Of course, sir; engaging FTL and heading in," replied the helmsman.

"Sounding clandestine stations," said the bosun, and he messaged the entire crew with orders to refrain from emitting anything that could be used to detect the ship—radio waves, radiation, anything at all.

"Good call, bosun. The warpers should, however, shield us from emitting anything that we do not want to emit," added the captain.

"The warp in space, however, would be unmistakable."

"I cannot argue with that."

The Shiny Moon entered Solar Empire space and raced to the objective. Even at high FTL speed, it still took two days for the ship to arrive at the target system. She dropped out of warp at the outermost edge and began to scan every single signal for signs of an Earth-like world.

"Found it, sir," relayed the head sensor officer.

"Good, transfer visual readout to the bridge," ordered the captain.

"Transferring," and the bridge officers began to view the results.

They saw a shiny blue marble; light wavelengths reflected from the atmosphere showed an estimated air composition of 76% nitrogen, 23% oxygen, and 1% trace gases—more or less a perfect copy of Earth's atmosphere. In addition, continents, massive oceans, and, more disturbingly, several large cities could also be viewed.

"Objective confirmed. Head sensor officer, relay the signal to the Admiralty. Priority emergency," ordered the captain, beginning the conspiracy.

"Yes, sir," replied the head sensor officer, and the signal was sent.

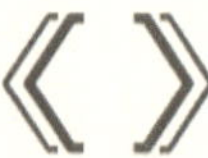

Back on Earth, a signal technician was eating his lunch. He was in charge of receiving any Emergency Quantum Entanglement signals from vessels assigned to special missions. A signal was received every couple of months if unlucky, and the signal technician merrily ate his lunch without a care. It was one of the best jobs that any sailor could hope to get in the navy. No work for years on end, and the computer alerts you with sound if a signal arrives.

Because of this, the unfortunate sailor spilled the contents of his lunch all over the counter and floor when the incredibly loud klaxon siren rang, alerting the signal technician that an Emergency Quantum Entanglement signal had just been received. The console printed out the message in a sealed tamper-resistant envelope and instructed the operator to deliver the note directly to Admiral Hackett, priority Sierra-H-56.

Cursing the fact that he would have to clean up the mess when he got back, he grabbed the note and raced out of the room. He went straight to the staircase of the Admiralty building and ran up the steps with such speed that he was panting like a marathon runner at the end of his run by the time he reached the Admiralty floor. He opened the door to the floor and was met by a sealed door, guarded by two sentinel soldiers.

"Sierra-H-56," said the signal technician, and the guards immediately opened the door and let him pass, knowing the meaning of such a priority code.

The signal technician raced to the desk of the naval secretary, the very same secretary who had greeted Captain Nagy and the Commodore when they arrived to see Admiral Hackett. She saw the young man arrive at a brisk pace.

"Yes, signal technician?" asked the naval secretary.

"I need to speak to Admiral Hackett urgently."

"He's in an important meeting and does not want to be disturbed."

"Sierra-H-56."

"I see, continue down the hall; his door is on the right-hand side."

"Thank you, Secretary." And the signal technician raced off.

He glanced at the name plaque on each door until he found one that he could not read because a Commodore with a full-service marine battle rifle was standing in front of it.

"Can I help you, signal technician?" asked the Commodore.

"Sierra-H-56."

"Go on in," said the Commodore, stepping aside.

The signal technician raced inside.

"Dammit, Richard, how many..." an Admiral stopped.

"A signal technician; you bring important news, I hope?" asked Admiral Hackett, who could not help but smile at the panting young man.

"Yes, sir. Emergency Quantum Entanglement signal, relayed to you personally. Priority Sierra-H-56," replied the signal technician in between gasps of breath as he handed Admiral Hackett the tamper-resistant envelope.

"Thank you, signal officer. Return to your post," ordered the Admiral, and the signal technician saluted and quickly left the room. The Commodore closed the door and returned to his sentry post immediately after.

The Admiral grabbed a special knife from his drawer and opened the note. Taking out the folded paper, he began to read.

"Shiny Moon. First objective system located, fully terraformed world verified and confirmed. Massive Solar Empire colonial and military presence detected. Confirmed sighting of Terraforming Installation; Solar Empire tried and failed to capture Terraforming Installation. Shiny Moon currently in pursuit of Terraforming Installation. Several Imperial Battlecruisers in pursuit of Shiny Moon."

The Admiral grinned broadly before speaking: "I told you that William would not disappoint." He handed the letter to the other two Admirals who were with him in the meeting.

The two Admirals read the note, and each one grinned as they digested its contents. Once the second Admiral handed the note back to Admiral Hackett, the direction of the meeting abruptly changed.

"I'll talk to my boys and get the party started," said one of the Admirals.

"I'll do the same," replied the other Admiral, and they both got up.

"I can't wait to see the look on the President's face!" remarked Admiral Hackett with a smile as the two Admirals left his office.

The Commodore closed the door and returned to his sentry position. Admiral Hackett pulled out a Quantum Entanglement Messenger Pad, one of the most expensive pieces of electronics in the galaxy, and started to send out orders to his carefully placed naval assets across Solar Empire space.

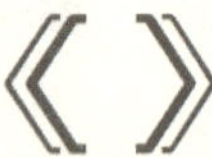

"Sir, Operation Liberation is a go. Orders just came in," relayed the head sensor officer of the Gravity Well through a live communications line.

The Gravity Well was nestled behind a large asteroid, deep in Solar Empire territory. She carried with her ten thousand refractively coated nuclear fusion warheads, and her target was a major Imperial shipyard planet.

"Alright, head gunnery officer, launch all warheads. Program them to prioritize enemy settlements, shipyards, and any lucky bastards who try to flee on their ships from the doomed world. Helmsman, once we are empty, maximum warp back to our space," ordered the Captain.

"Yes, sir!" replied the head gunnery officer through the line.

"Engines hot and ready to warp," added the helmsman.

The Gravity Well quickly emerged from behind the asteroid and opened her payload doors. The warheads each contained a dozen individual hydrogen bombs, with a blast yield of one hundred megatons each. With the ten thousand refractively coated fusion nuclear warheads currently loaded aboard ship, her total firepower in terms of individual hydrogen bombs numbered one hundred and twenty thousand—enough to easily destroy a target planet.

"Beginning launch." After a few seconds, the head gunnery officer said, "Launching!"

The ship vibrated as the hundreds of specialized railguns began to hurl the warheads toward the target planet at incredible speeds. The ship began to move in the opposite direction, such was the force of the recoil from the railguns as they quickly depleted the stockpile of warheads through their rapid fire. In just under three minutes, all ten thousand warheads were launched, heading straight for the target planet.

Once in range, the warheads will open and scatter the dozen individual bombs across the atmosphere. A few will enter temporary orbits, looping around the planet in search of juicy targets. Others will punch through the atmosphere and smack into the planet without any delay, while others still will skim the atmosphere, hunting for fleeing ships that try to escape. In the end, all warheads not shot down will detonate on the planet, dooming the world for many centuries.

If all goes well for the defenders, twenty thousand of the warheads will be shot down; the other hundred thousand, however, will be more than enough to successfully complete the objective.

"Warheads away, engaging FTL," said the helmsman, and the Gravity Well entered warp and fled, leaving her target world to its certain fate.

Such an event was being repeated all across the Solar Empire. Carefully selected targets, the fruit of decades of careful intelligence and analysis, all leading up to this moment. The crews were handpicked down to the janitor for loyalty and secrecy. By the time the truth emerged, the Republic of Earth would be in a state of total war and too busy to care.

"Captain, I think we lost them this time," said the helmsman of the Shiny Moon.

"You think?" replied the captain.

"We've been evading them for over a month, we used nearly all of our warp decoys, and frankly, we've done so many FTL maneuvers that even I am confused. If I were betting all in, I would bet it all on the fact that we lost them."

"Very well, helmsman. Bosun, sound down combat stations."

"Yes, captain," replied the bosun, and combat stations were turned off.

"Everyone take a few hours' break. Once the break is over, return to the bridge and prepare to set the destination to the next solar system. Officers' meeting at 18:00 ship time," ordered the captain, and everyone wasted no time in starting to enjoy their few hours of respite.

The Shiny Moon was busy confirming all of the suspected leads that the dossier had provided. So far, they had confirmed six systems; each one had a fully terraformed world, complete with a sizable Solar Empire presence. Lately, massive FTL warp signals could be detected all across nearby space; all the signals had the same heading: Republic of Earth space. Whatever Admiral Hackett did with the message that the Shiny Moon sent, it definitely angered the hornet's nest.

A staffer for the President was racing with yet another intelligence update, wasting no time in getting to the emergency meeting that President Varis had convened. The staffer raced in, handed the intelligence update to one of the generals, and left as soon as she had arrived.

"Do we know why?" asked the President, who still could not process the reports that were coming in—a massive invasion by the Solar Empire across all border and frontier systems.

"Frankly, sir, they think we are weak. Much of our military force, after all, had been mothballed for over a decade, and they likely thought that now was the best time to pounce in the form of a surprise attack if they wished to obtain a quick and total victory in war," replied Admiral Hackett, who was seated with the rest of the Admiralty to the right of the President.

"I concur with the Navy; all our boys have been merrily drinking and whoring since the start of mothball. Any spy who is not a complete and utter fool is going to relay nothing but good news once he is debriefed after the conclusion of his mission," added one of the senior generals.

"So, in the time that it'll take to bring everyone out of mothball, we are more or less defenseless?" asked the President, who was beginning to regret several decisions that he had made throughout his long political career.

"Not exactly, sir," replied Admiral Hackett, who handed the President a special report.

The President took the report and started to read; his face went red with anger and then started to mellow slightly as he finished the report.

"You military bastards have been secretly building an armada of ships and armies since the start of mothball. All those delays and problems with my domestic projects? That was all the military stealing funds and resources away," hissed President Varis, the betrayal still stinging in his chest.

"Sir, every sailor and soldier in this room swore an oath. *We swear to defend the Republic against all enemies, foreign and domestic. We shall do so through any tribulation, great or small, until we breathe our last breath.* We saw the writing on the wall from the start, and each soldier and sailor here worked to guard the Republic that we all love against a tribulation that was sure to come. Had we followed your example, the war would already be lost," said one of the generals.

"From what this report tells me, we have a very large armada of ships and hundreds of millions of soldiers in the army, with all the gear needed to invade worlds. Where are they all right now?" asked the President.

"Regarding the navy, a quarter is currently swinging around and striking targets of opportunity throughout Solar Empire space to throw off the enemy and force them to divert a portion of their invading force to chase our raiding forces. The other is holding firm at the beginning of the frontier. The frontier worlds are strategically worthless, with a minimal population. Sacrificing them to the Solar Empire will buy us time, a week or two at most. That, combined with the raiders in their space, will give us enough time to mobilize the mothballed ships and soldiers and have them join our hidden force," replied Admiral Hackett.

"And will that be enough to drive the invaders back?"

"We cannot guarantee that, but it will give us a good chance of doing so. There is one final thing that I suggest, Mr. President. We convert the economy to a total war economy as soon as possible. Nationalize all industry and force it to produce ships, weapons, and gear for combat, as well as redirect all of our best minds and workers to the development and production of advanced weaponry. Every citizen of the Republic needs to do their part, whether serving in conscription or working in the factory at home, while rationing as much as they can."

"Politically, that will be impossible," said the President.

"Not really, sir," replied Admiral Hackett.

"Why not?"

"Remember the holding back of our forces right at the start of the frontier? We have already discussed reports in this very meeting that show the indiscriminate bombing of our frontier worlds with nuclear weapons. No care as to potential civilian casualties; we even received satellite video of the deliberate targeting of city settlements."

"You want us to broadcast this across the Republic?"

"Exactly, Mr. President. Every news broadcast, every single personal computer should be blaring these images, sounds, and reports until the end of the war. The sacrifice of our frontier does not just buy us time to get the rest of our forces out of mothball, but it also allows us to justify the establishment of total war. No one will question your judgment."

"Very well, let us continue the meeting then; we have much to discuss."

"That we do, sir."

A month into the war, the two sides had started to find themselves in a stalemate. The Solar Empire had no problem with the Republic of Earth's frontier; it folded and was conquered and destroyed in just under a week. Once they started to touch the outermost band of Republic of Earth space, however, everything changed. The clandestine navy, combined with a sizable portion of the reactivated mothball fleet, decisively defeated the main invading fleet at the Battle of Houtilinia IV.

The war now entered a fluid stalemate, with the brunt of the fighting taking place on the frontier worlds of the Republic of Earth, with some spillover into Solar Empire space. The two sides began to mobilize every possible sailor, soldier, and resource that they could lay their hands on.

Chapter Nine

"Attention all hands, we are approaching the target system."

Captain Nagy woke up to the sound of the bosun's call and quickly got dressed before he exited his quarters. Racing to the captain's chair, he sat down and was eager to begin his day.

"Distance, bosun?" he asked.

"Around five minutes at current FTL velocity."

"Good."

The ship closed in on the objective, and after five minutes, it dropped out of FTL at the edge of the system. The crew got to work scanning the system immediately for anything of interest.

"Interesting," relayed the head sensor officer through a live wire.

"Please elaborate, head sensor officer," pressed the captain.

"In the other six systems that we have visited, we had to run away without any delay because of the significant Solar Empire presence."

"And this system is empty?"

"Exactly, Captain, not a single Solarian in sight."

"Helmsman, what do the astronautical charts say?"

"We should still be deep in their space."

"Perhaps they have not bothered to colonize this system yet," said the captain out loud, clearly wanting others on the bridge to add their two cents.

"Captain, if I may," added the first officer.

"You always may, first officer. Speak your mind."

"It is logical to presume that the Solar Empire has the most valuable worlds and assets close to heart. Having them spread out across their space would be a very foolish decision in the event of war. This truth, combined with the fact that they are no doubt in a serious war with our Republic, means only one thing: the worlds were hastily colonized."

"Agreed on the hastily colonized part," added the captain.

"The other six worlds were colonized quickly, but the dossier tells us that there are dozens of worlds. Furthermore, the worlds themselves seem to be located in very remote areas—either hiding in plain sight, as the first system near the border between the Solar Empire and our Republic was, or in far-flung areas, which we are still trying to decipher."

"Alright, let us use this opportunity to the fullest. Helmsman, take us in and have us orbit the habitable world," ordered the captain.

"How close, sir, and what orbit type?" asked the helmsman.

"Close, around 250-300 miles above the surface, and have the orbit be elliptical."

"Understood, sir."

The Shiny Moon activated her sub-light torch engines and approached the habitable world. She reached the world quickly and entered an elliptical orbit at a distance of 260 miles from the surface.

"Do we have any scientific equipment onboard, other than the sensors?" asked the captain of the different ship departments. They all replied in the negative.

"Head sensor officer, our sensors can gather a diverse amount of data, no?" asked the captain.

"Thousands of different types of data, sir."

"Good, start scanning the world in every single possible way that we can. If anything of interest is found, notify me immediately."

"Yes, sir."

"Head doctor, you have a biology background, correct?"

"I can be a junior scientist if that is what you are implying."

The captain hesitated for a moment before responding, his mind deep in thought. After this slight delay, he smiled and gave his response.

"Your decontamination chamber, tell me it still works."

"Of course, why do you..." The head officer stopped; he knew why.

"If we go to the surface and gather organic samples, do you think that the medical devices we have onboard could be repurposed for science?"

"They more than likely could, captain."

"Good, go and assemble a team. I'll join you in the shuttle bay."

"Yes, captain."

The captain sat back in his chair and grinned, his mind wild with ideas.

"Captain?" asked the first officer.

"Yes, first officer?" replied the captain.

"This is a bad idea, but then again, you're going to do it anyway."

"Right on both points, as usual," replied the captain with a smile.

The captain spent a few more moments on the bridge before relinquishing control to his first officer as he headed out toward the shuttle bay. He took the elevator down to the shuttle deck and walked toward the location of the shuttles at the back of the ship. He entered a small preparation room, where the head doctor and several of his colleagues were donning biological isolation suits.

"Captain, a pleasure," said the head doctor.

"A pleasure indeed, head doctor. Where's my suit?"

"Right here." The head doctor pointed to a small box on top of a table.

Captain Nagy went over to the table and opened the box. He took out the durable plastic isolation suit and put it on. Taking several minutes, he checked the air seal; it was airtight against the outside atmosphere.

"Alright, let us gather as much life as possible—plants, insects, and if possible, a small creature. Anything that appears to be dangerous, dispatch and recover with a rifle," ordered the captain, who pointed to a rack of rifles on the wall.

The amateur scientific team all grabbed a rifle alongside the rest of their gear, and they made their way to one of the shuttles. After securing the gear and rifles inside the shuttle, the pilot, who was waiting for them, walked over to the shuttle and entered the cockpit through the open canopy. He, like the rest of the team, also wore a biological isolation suit.

"Pilot, keep the engines hot and ready to depart. Make sure that an open line is maintained with the ship at all times, starting now," ordered the captain.

"Yes, sir. Opening and maintaining an open communication line."

"Bridge, do you read?" asked the captain.

"Loud and clear, captain," replied the bosun.

"I want you to drop a signal amplifier behind you as you orbit. That way, the pilot and the team can keep in touch with you even if the ship is on the other side of the planet."

"Yes, sir. Dropping now."

"Perfect; in that case, see you in a short while, Shiny Moon."

"Roger that. Be safe, captain."

"Alright, pilot, get us to the surface," ordered the captain.

"Yes, sir!"

The pilot requested the shuttle bay doors to be opened after bay depressurization, and after a few moments, the doors opened, and the shuttle roared off into space. The planet up ahead was beautiful, filled with vibrant green, white, and blue colors. There were several large oceans, combined with inland seas, a few islands, and decently sized continents. More or less just like Earth, of course, with radically different landmass shapes and ocean placements.

The shuttle began to glow as it hit the packed atmosphere, and after around ten minutes of descent, the shuttle stabilized and landed on a grass field surrounded by woodland. A great flock of birds scattered in all directions as the shuttle landed, and bugs immediately began to pour in as the shuttle doors opened. The air filled with the sounds of buzzing and chirping.

"The samples are coming to us!" said one of the junior medics.

"Collect the samples quickly, and don't dilly-dally!" hissed the head doctor.

"Of course, sir!"

The bugs that entered the shuttle were quickly collected and stored in various bins and vials. The team began to step outside and collect samples from any and all plants scattered on the field. Dozens of different flowering plants, ferns, and other plant life could be found on the ground. The team did not waste any time gathering them.

The captain did not participate in the sampling; instead, his gaze was focused on the distant tree line. They landed in a climate that seemed too dry to be a rainforest; instead, the feel of the land appeared to be similar to that of the forests back on Earth, which were located in the middle between the equator and the respective pole of the hemisphere in which the forest was located.

Eyeing a resting bird, the captain aimed his rifle and took a shot. The bullet, designed to penetrate hostile borders in armored space suits, brutally tore through the bird, leaving it a mangled carcass alongside a temporary puff of feathers. The captain walked over to the bird, picked up the remains, and then walked back, placing the bloody carcass inside one of the sample bins.

"Smart thinking. It's hard to tell what kind of bird it is at a glance, but I'm sure the DNA testing will tell us more," quipped the head doctor, seeing the mess that the captain made.

"I forgot that these rifles are loaded with ripper rounds," replied the captain.

"I, for one, am happy. If we get the mutated form of a hippopotamus charging at us, I want a magazine filled with rippers to keep me safe," replied the head doctor.

"No argument there."

The captain continued to scan the tree line for threats, acting as a sentry for the group. After half an hour, the team had gathered nearly all of the observable organisms that could be found in the grass field around the shuttle.

"I suggest entering the woodland and hunting for some more samples, Captain," suggested one of the junior medics on the team.

"Better chance of finding more advanced life," added the head doctor.

"And the ripper rounds would do nicely against predators. I agree; proceed, everyone," ordered the captain, and the team moved into the woodland.

"Pilot, give us a hand with your scanners," ordered the captain through radio communication.

"Of course, anything in particular?" asked the pilot quickly.

"Movement from anything that is the size of a man."

"I see; I can give general heat signatures."

"That's good enough. If the temperature in a certain area starts to go up, do let us know."

"Will do, Captain."

The crew hugged the woodland; this time, the captain was joined by two others in his sentry duty, the three vigilantly scanning the woods ahead with rifles in hand. Of particular value to the team were the great varieties of mushrooms that sprouted from decaying tree trunks that had fallen onto the forest floor. More insect varieties were gathered, and the respective bins and vials were starting to get full.

"Alright, Captain, we have plenty of samples to get a rough genetic makeup of the different types of life on this world," replied the head doctor.

"Back to the shuttle," ordered the captain, and the team obeyed.

They arrived at the shuttle, and the pilot spoke with the Shiny Moon, requesting a return vector. One was given; however, the shuttle would have to wait an hour before departing the world in order to meet up with the ship.

"An hour is survivable," hissed one of the junior medics.

"Wait, this reminds me, did we use the Petri dishes?" asked the captain.

"No, sir, we did not!" replied another junior medic.

"Then we can spend a portion of the hour sampling the most important, and arguably the most dangerous, organism on this rock!"

"Indeed, Captain." The junior medic started to unpack the dishes.

"I'll stand guard; bacteria are notorious for slipping past even the best defenses," added the captain, and the junior medic let out a giggle.

An hour had passed, and with a full stockpile of biological samples, the shuttle was ready to return to the Shiny Moon. The pilot wasted no time in confirming the return vector.

"Shiny Moon, this is shuttle. We good to go?"

"Yes, shuttle. Come on home."

"Roger."

The pilot roared off, rapidly gaining altitude as the grassy field faded away. After a quarter hour, the shuttle was in space, approaching a faint object that quickly came into view as the Shiny Moon.

The shuttle slowed down and turned in order to match the shuttle bay entrance. Slowly but surely, the shuttle eased in and latched onto the shuttle deck with powerful magnetic clamps. The bay was pressurized with air, and once at normal Earth atmosphere pressure, a team of decontamination specialists, dressed in the same biological isolation suits as the shuttle team, arrived. They took the samples, sealed them in heavy see-through plastic crates, and after giving the cart a mighty spray, wheeled it toward the medical quarantine laboratory on the medical deck.

The same was done to the shuttle, both the inside and the outside, as well as the arriving team. The shuttle team waited until the shuttle deck was thoroughly sprayed with disinfectant; it would later be depressurized and exposed to space, followed by a sustained dose of extremely high levels of radiation, enough to kill even the most resistant organism known to man.

Once the decontamination specialists finished their work, they, alongside the decontamination team, went to the airlock that separated the shuttle bay from the preparation room. They were saturated with disinfecting agents and had to stay in place for over an hour; this was the replacement form of decontamination in lieu of decompression and radiation saturation. Once the hour was over, everyone rushed into the preparation room and took off their biological isolation suits.

"Finally, I was cooking alive in there!" complained a junior medic.

"You did well, son," said the captain with a smile, patting the junior medic on the shoulder.

"Thank you, sir; I greatly appreciate that."

The captain started to take off his disinfected biological suit, but before he could finish, he heard a sound: "Captain, a moment," said the bosun from one of the speakers on the wall.

"Yes, bosun?"

"We need you on the bridge immediately; there has been a development. One that I believe you do not want to miss."

"I'll be there right away."

Once he took off the disinfected biological suit and straightened out his uniform, the captain left the preparation room and walked the shuttle deck toward the elevator. He entered it, pressed the button that directed it to go to the bridge deck, and he went straight to the bridge deck without pause.

Once he arrived at the bridge, he returned to his chair, sat down, and regained command from his first officer. The message from the bosun had his mind racing.

"Alright, tell me about this development," pleaded the captain.

"It is better if you listen to it, sir," replied the bosun.

The bosun played the development out loud. It was a series of beeps and clicks, followed by audio. The audio was somewhat comprehensible, but it sounded strange and wrong. The captain focused on it until he understood the problem.

"The specific language—it is ancient!" the captain said in surprise.

"Indeed, from the days of the Human Unity," replied the bosun.

"I hear it talking about a journey, but I can't comprehend the rest."

"We've translated it while you were off on your little safari; take a look on your computer, sir."

The captain pulled up the display on his console and began to read:

"Vessel from Earth that pursues me, rest your tired engines and listen to my words. You will not find me among the children that I have created. If you seek such knowledge, you must travel far to the end of Perseus's arm. There, among the few of you who remain free, you will find a vessel, the Jalalight. On board is a crew of free men; they have the answers you seek."

The captain finished reading the message and was puzzled and angry.

"It's teasing us," he spat out in anger.

"That, or this is a ruse from the Solar Empire," added the first officer.

"Bosun, search our computer database for any ship that flies a nomad flag under the name of Jalalight," asked the captain.

The bosun took a few moments before answering, "Negative, sir."

"Great. Still, why waste time with a ruse if this is the Solar Empire? No specific destination; finding a ship at the end of the galactic arm is the only way this can be effective in terms of strategy—to steer us off course," added the captain.

"Agreed, Captain. They likely suspect that we know of the terraformed worlds, and by having us on a goose chase, they hope to keep us distracted. Maybe the answers we seek are in the other systems that we have yet to visit," suggested the first officer.

"Where is the signal coming from, Bosun?"

"The nearby asteroid belt. Dammit, Captain, you are smart."

"Damn straight, Bosun. Helmsman, set course for the signal. I want whatever is broadcasting it. Before I forget, sound battle stations, Bosun."

"Yes, sir!" replied the helmsman.

"Yes, sir!" replied the bosun.

The ship, cocooned in a protective shield and with her railguns and missiles live and ready for use, raced toward the source of the signal. As the ship got closer, it was determined that the signal was transmitting from a specific asteroid of medium size.

"Anything that screams I'm going to shoot you?" asked the captain.

"Negative, sir. Seems like any old space rock," replied the head sensor officer through an open communications line.

"Send in an RCS drone; find me that transmitter."
"Yes, Captain."
The sensor team sent out an RCS scout drone toward the asteroid.

Chapter Ten

"So far, so good, Captain. Nothing but asteroids ahead of us," relayed the head sensor officer.

"Carry on," replied the captain.

The drone inched closer to the asteroid and began to orbit it in a scan pattern once it got close enough. Nothing was detected that was out of the ordinary, and the drone continued to orbit until it detected a cavern in the asteroid. Ordered to investigate, it went in and found the transmitter.

"The transmitter is not that large; we can take it out with the drone," said the head sensor officer.

"Proceed," replied the captain.

Taking out the transmitter slowly and with a delicate touch, the drone paused halfway between the asteroid and the ship, allowing the sensor team to get a good scan and analyze the transmitter before bringing it aboard.

"Looks good, sir," said the head sensor officer.

"Bring it in and give me a report," replied the captain.

"Yes, sir."

The head sensor officer followed the captain's order and brought the transmitter into one of the small cargo bays. A technician team raced to the cargo bay in order to analyze it.

"Helmsman, assuming we head straight for the end of Perseus's arm, how many terraformed systems are there between our current location and the end of the arm?" asked the captain.

"One second, sir." The helmsman took several moments before responding, "Two."

"Assuming general FTL velocity, how long until we reach the end of the arm?"

"Four to seven months, sir."

"Alright, set course for the first of the two solar systems. First officer, you have the bridge. I'm going to go have a word with our civilian liaison about the extension of service contracts."

"Understood, sir."

The captain got up from the chair and left the bridge, taking the elevator down to the civilian decks. Assuming that the civilian liaison's office was in the same place as it was a decade ago, he went directly there.

"Captain, looking nice today!" called out one of the civilians.

"He always looks nice," replied another civilian.

Unable to contain his grin, the captain continued to walk toward the civilian liaison's office. The corridors were filled with civilians and off-duty sailors, each one eagerly wanting what the other had. The sailors wanted some stimulation, while the civilians wanted their currency. Everyone seemed happy.

Seeing that the door to the civilian liaison's office was closed, the captain tapped the bulkhead door with his knuckles. A moment passed before there was a response.

"Yes? Who is it?" asked the voice of Ensign Nicole.

"Captain William Nagy. Do you have a moment?"

"Of course, Captain. Please come in!"

The captain opened the bulkhead door and entered. Inside the room, Ensign Nicole was seated behind her desk, with several civilians in front of it. They seemed to be frustrated about something.

"You sure about not being busy?"

"Yes, in fact, I might as well brief you now."

President Varis was furious, and as soon as the Admiralty that was summoned to his office walked in, he began to let it all out without any mercy.

"I know," said President Varis plainly, his rage building up.

"I do not understand what you mean, sir?" replied Admiral Hackett.

"Don't be coy, you bastard. You attacked the Solar Empire first."

"Attacked? In what..."

"Don't deny it!" yelled the President, who grabbed a dossier and threw it at the Admiral, hitting him square in the left shoulder.

"Pick it up. You will tell me why before I have you all shot!"

Admiral Hackett looked at the scattered pages of reports and images, and he knew that the gig was up. However, he did not feel like bending down and picking up the scattered documents, especially not at the order of someone he so despises.

"You threw it; why don't you pick it up?" retorted Admiral Hackett.

"How dare you! The whole miserable lot of you start a war, and then you all think that you are some big shots, able to disregard your places? I am sorry, I spoke too soon; after all, you all have been stripped of your respective ranks," hissed the Secretary of Defense.

Admiral Hackett pulled out his Quantum Entanglement Messenger Pad, and immediately the Secretary of Defense rushed him. He went straight for the pad, hoping to break it before the Admiral could send out a signal. However, the Secretary of Defense, who had spent a lifetime in public service, did not have the speed nor the strength to fend off several seasoned sailors, who promptly subdued him.

The President immediately reached for the panic button under his desk. He had a smile on his face as he pressed it before returning to his previous stance as the commotion in his office began to die down; hundreds of soldiers, after all, would be swarming his office in mere moments.

"So, a coup d'état in my own office?" asked the President.

Admiral Hackett ignored the President as he sent out a message. "Liberate the land; it is finally time." It was a simple message, and it was sent to a single recipient. Message sent, he returned to the business at hand.

"I apologize for the delay in answering you, Mr. President; I had to send a message, as you can clearly see." The Admiral put away the pad as he spoke. "No, this is not a coup d'état; it's insulting of you to suggest such a thing."

"Then what is this, Admiral?" asked the President, who was more than happy to have the Admiral talk for as long as he wanted, at least until the soldiers arrived to respond to the panic button press.

"Mind if I take a seat? I don't think your Secretary of Defense is using this chair at the moment?" asked Admiral Hackett, who took a seat even before the President could give an answer.

"Why ask if you are just going to do it?"

"Good question, Mr. President; I reckon the answer is politeness."

"Politeness? Dammit, Admiral, why did you do it? The Solar Empire was simply too big of a potential enemy to allow to live in peace?"

"Indeed, but the Solar Empire was not the only reason. You see, our republic has been infected with a great infestation, Mr. President—an infestation that has severely corrupted not only our governmental bureaucracy but also our way of life. Do you remember the oath that you swore when you entered this office?" asked Admiral Hackett with a smile.

"The one that you are currently breaking, Admiral? Of course."

"Good. Firstly, I do not like to have sensitive conversations eavesdropped on by outside parties," said Admiral Hackett while looking at the Secretary of Defense.

Those restraining him understood the order, and they twisted his tie until it was at the back of his neck and began to pull hard, strangling him.

"This one was always an annoyance. Imagine having to see his face every single day, knowing that he was a traitor, and yet not being able to do a single thing about it," added Admiral Hackett as the Secretary of Defense squirmed and yelled.

The President did not move, but he was cursing the incompetence and laziness of the soldiers who should have responded by now. He made a note to demand several resignation letters once they finally arrived.

"Absolutely pathetic, sir. The fact that this traitor here is apparently your friend, but you will not do a thing to try and save him?" Admiral Hackett paused and looked at the Secretary of Defense. Even though he had stopped moving, the other admirals did not relent on the strangulation. One of them had a finger on his neck, counting the heartbeats.

The President had a face of hatred but did not respond.

"Ah, I see. You are waiting for the soldiers who are coming because of that little button that you pressed? Is my assumption correct?"

The President did not respond; his face started to go pale.

"Thank you for confirming it. I'm sorry that I did not get to this part sooner in our conversation, but the soldiers that are coming—well, let us say that they are going to be slightly delayed."

The President did not respond; instead, he jumped out of his chair and more or less broke one of his desk drawers as he opened it. He grabbed a pistol that he kept, and with trembling hands, squeezed the trigger as fast as he could while aiming it directly at Admiral Hackett's chest.

"Click. Click. Click. Click. Click." The clicks stopped as the President's hands started to shake violently and uncontrollably.

"You want to know what I dislike the most about you? Tell me, when was the last time that you serviced your sidearm? What about the last time that you took her out on the range? Made her squeal with delight as you lubricated her barrel? It must have been months—no doubt years—since you have done any of those things. Most importantly, in your situation, when was the last time that you checked her magazine?"

The President threw the pistol onto the table in anger; it hit, bounced off the table, and landed on the floor. The Admiral was furious at the sight.

"And now you discard her, after years of neglect—shameful."

"I'm tired of this! If you have any demands that you—"

The President screamed as the bullet ripped through his left upper leg. The round was a ripper round, pistol caliber, but still enough to cause a grievous injury. The bullet pulverized the President's femur and severed his femoral artery. The semi-intact leg began to lose blood at an alarming rate.

"My pistol, on the other hand, is spoiled rotten. Every other day at a minimum, she is out on the range. Sometimes I feed her only a few shots; other times, she is given hundreds of bullets to feast upon. She is serviced daily, and her chamber is as clean as the silverware that you are given each and every day for your Presidential dinner. Finally, I know how many rounds are in my magazine at all times: eight, plus one in the chamber. I have eight rounds remaining—one in the chamber, seven in the magazine."

The President resigned himself to his fate. He did not bother responding; he simply lay limp until the blood loss made him lose consciousness. He then died a few minutes later. Admiral Hackett got up and took a seat in the still-warm Presidential chair. It was comfortable, a chair that he had worked tirelessly for over a decade to sit in.

"Orders, Mr. President?" asked one of the Admirals, who all in unison saluted their new commanding officer.

"Bring in the 'panic' response team. Have them drag these two spineless politicians out," said President Hackett.

"Right away, sir." The Admiral left the President's office.

"In the meantime, we need to wait to see the results of our special forces teams. Hopefully, they manage to intercept and eliminate all the other Secretaries before the idiots realize what is going on," said President Hackett with a grin.

"I have no doubt that our men will succeed, sir," said another Admiral.

"Only time will tell, Admiral. In the meantime, organize a war meeting. Have the Admirals and Generals meet us in three hours. I have a few things that I need to do first, and several of them will need convincing of our most recent change in government."

"Leave that to us, Mr. President. In three hours, you will have a unified military, ready and willing for you to give the order to crush the Solarian scum once and for all."

"I like the sound of that. Dismissed."

For the next three hours, the military brass that conspired with Admiral Hackett to overthrow the government painstakingly worked to convince the last remnants among the upper echelons of the military that the newly appointed President was just what the republic needed at this most perilous time. As expected, the vast majority refused to have anything to do with this, and they were quickly executed and replaced with loyal officers.

The last of the old military guard now removed, the Admiralty and Generalcy informed President Hackett that he had a unified military. Eager to remove the 'stalemate' farce that he had to dangle in front of the President, he arrived at the meeting several minutes early. Everyone else had already done the same thing.

"Well, it seems that we are all eager to begin!" said President Hackett.

"I have to say, Mr. President, seeing you in a suit is a shock to my eyes. It looks good on you," replied one of the Generals.

"I was as shocked as you are right now when I saw it in the mirror."

"Indeed, sir. I'm sure that you will accustom yourself quickly to it."

"I hope so, General. Alright, let us not waste any time; the previous administration, controlled by weak-spined, traitorous bastards who let our soldiers and sailors rot away for over a decade, has finally been removed. It took us a very long time to do so; for that, I apologize."

"No need, sir. If we had moved any sooner, the chance of failure would have been too high to be acceptable," added one of the Admirals.

"We all know and agree with that, Admiral. Still, every single day that I saw my sailors and marines rotting on the streets, drinking, whoring, and drugging themselves to death, was another day of misery for me."

"Not just for you, for all of us, sir."

"Indeed, Admiral, indeed."

"Speaking of whoring, how's that all-important vessel, the one that confirmed the existence of the Terraforming Installation?" asked one of the generals, which caused the room to erupt in laughter for a moment.

"The Shiny Moon?" asked an admiral.

"Aye, that's the one," replied the general.

"We haven't heard from her in months, ever since the war started. The last transmission we received was immediately after she confirmed the existence of the Terraforming Installation. They had arrived at one of the terraformed systems and saw the Terraforming Installation briefly before it fled in FTL. They messaged us that they were in direct pursuit, with several Solarian bogeys on their tail," added President Hackett.

"Hmm, and not a peep since?" asked the general.

"Not a one. We unfortunately assume that the Solarians either captured or destroyed her at the beginning of the war. There is, however, some hope; the quantum entanglement bond has not suffered any major disruptions. Either the ship was destroyed and, miraculously, the interstellar communications suite was more or less preserved intact, or she is still alive and kicking," replied the President.

"Alright, let's go with the assumption that she was lost with all hands. We need to find the Terraforming Installation," said the general.

"Agreed. Luckily, we can finally use the full force of our navy. Assuming half of the reserve force that we never mentioned to the previous President is used against the forces currently invading our borders, what are the chances of victory?" asked the President.

"With just half? I reckon 75%, Mr. President," replied an admiral; the rest of the admirals agreed with her estimate.

"Very well, in that case, allocate 80% of the new naval force to our current defenders. The other 20%, I want them sent directly into Solar Empire space. The remnant of our existing raiding force, combined with the most advanced ships that we have ever designed in the history of our republic, should be enough to bring the Solarian industrial capacity to heel. And best of all, we decimate their navy at the same time with the rest of our forces," said the President with a smile.

"A much better stance than the previous President, I must say," replied a general, and the room cheered in agreement.

"I try," said the President with a tease.

"Alright, I know that this is somewhat premature, but we need to discuss the future of this republic when we defeat the Solar Empire. I suggest that we completely and utterly destroy them, sparing only the most valuable worlds for future settlement, resource extraction, or industrial production. Of course, assuming that any of them survive the conquest," added an admiral.

"It is not premature at all. My goal has always been to get our sailors and soldiers out of mothball, make sure that our military is the strongest in the known galaxy, and finally, ensure that the nuisance known as the Solar Empire is destroyed. I have not thought about what comes next," replied the President.

"I suggest, Mr. President, that we reform the republic, not for a while, perhaps in a year or three," said the admiral.

"Reform? How?" asked the President.

"The Solar Empire, once conquered, is going to need an iron fist of repression to keep them down. Republics that hold constant elections are not exactly known for their iron fists. We need to fix that," replied the admiral.

Chapter Eleven

"You know me; I love my briefings," said Captain Nagy, who walked over to one of the empty chairs in front of Ensign Nicole's desk and sat down.

"The ladies are getting, well, restless waiting for news about the end of their enlistments. We have been warping around the galaxy, buzzing like bees. The sailors are telling the girls that we are in some sort of war, and the civilians are getting nervous. Now that you are here, I believe that you can alleviate their concerns with news straight from the mouth of the highest-ranking officer aboard the ship," replied Ensign Nicole.

"I see. I'll be glad to alleviate your concerns. Do you ladies mind sharing the information that you hear here today with the rest of the girls?" asked the captain.

"Of course, Captain," replied one of the civilians.

"Perfect. In that case, tell me what the main concern is regarding your enlistments; I will answer them to the best of my ability."

"Are we at war?" asked one of the girls.

"We have not received direct confirmation, but more likely than not, based on evidence that we have seen, yes, we are at war."

"With whom?" she pressed.

"The Solar Empire."

"What the hell happened?" asked another civilian.

"The Solar Empire decided to expand her territory, in my opinion."

"You don't know, do you?"

"You are correct; I do not know the exact reason for the war."

"So, about our contracts; we have to extend them, no?"

"Yes, that is actually why I'm here."

Ensign Nicole smiled. "Double pay for everyone; I doubt that the girls would mind. Would you?" she asked, turning to face the civilians.

"Double pay plus the business from the sailors is good money. The problem is spending it; there is nothing aboard ship that one can spend it on, and now with the war, when are we going to get shore leave?" replied one of the civilians.

"Several months at the absolute minimum. However, if fortune blesses us, you all will get the chance to spend your hoard of credits in around six to eight months. Maybe more, maybe less," said the captain.

"Alright, I'll spread the word around; worst-case scenario, Captain, your boys are going to be light in their pockets by the time the mission is over. Let us give the captain and the liaison some privacy," said the civilian, and she and the other girls left the room, closing the bulkhead door behind them.

"She was always a feisty one," said Ensign Nicole.

"Oh? How long have you known her?" asked Captain Nagy with a smile.

"A few years; never wanted for work until a few months back. She is a lion dining on gazelles aboard this ship. Then again, the gazelles cannot seem to get enough of her; they always come back."

"Honestly, at this point I'd rather have my men spend their credits on the women rather than on drinks and drugs that corrode their bodies and discipline."

"That apply to the captain too?" teased Nicole.

"Don't start; I don't have any credits in my pockets."

"We'll just put it on your tab." Nicole started to unbutton her dress shirt, revealing a portion of her upper cleavage.

"And to think that such an act would normally have you court-martialed and jailed. How the times change," remarked the captain with a smile.

Nicole and the captain spent the better part of an hour in passion. Finally remembering the objective for his visit to the liaison's office, the captain broke the hour of passion with a question regarding logistics.

"Paying the civilians is going to be a problem," said the captain.

"Dammit, you're right, especially since hard currency is becoming increasingly scarce aboard ship," replied Nicole, who was clearly informed as to the problem.

"I see. Run into this issue with any of your clients?"

"Aye, a few officer regulars of mine are starting to run low on credit chips. I am starting to accept tab debts in lieu of hard chips, but that is only a temporary solution. Now, with the extensions, we need to get people paid."

"I was thinking of requesting a quantum-backed crypto-credit transfer. The problem is getting the crypto converted into regular credits is a massive annoyance, as I'm sure you know," said the captain with a little pinch.

"Dammit, you just had to bring it up, you bastard!"

"I remember it clear as day. I was resting in my new apartment, freshly mothballed. I decided to get myself something nice for the night. I went through the catalog for local girls and came across this one girl; she seemed like a literal ballbuster in every sense of the word. Her name was Nicole."

"She is one, especially when one does not watch his words."

"Anyways, I messaged her, saying I'd like an hour. It took only ten minutes. Considering that I was fresh from deployment, it was to be expected. I went to pay her in the new quantum-backed crypto-credit currency that the Navy had unveiled. It was able to be used anywhere in the universe thanks to quantum entanglement, a perfect solution for paying sailors who wouldn't get back home to solid ground for many months or even years."

"And when you try to exchange it for regular credits, a 40% transaction fee!"

"I swore it was a Solarian hit squad when I heard you banging on my door. What was it, three or so in the morning?"

"More like four."

"Very well, four in the morning. I opened the door, and you gave me an earful. You accused me of scamming you. I had no idea what you were talking about until I made a few calls, then I realized the problem."

"You took me out for dinner and paid for two hours of company, a true gentleman," said Nicole with a smile.

"Oh, I got my money's worth during those two hours. I remember it well; the sun just started to come out when our session wrapped up. I have to say, Nicole, I would not have made it through a decade of mothball without you. In another life, we would be married, farming on some frontier world."

"And have the farm burned to a crisp by raiders."

"Aye, it doesn't sound as good when I think about it a second time," admitted the captain, who gave the ensign a kiss on the cheek.

"What a wild ride my life has been, and I admit, it would not have been the same without you, William."

"I have no doubt, with the amount of money that I gave you over the years."

"Ah hush, the money was good; you, however, were even better."

The pair continued to cuddle and reminisce about old times. The moment was passionate and strong, interrupted only by a knock on the door.

"Yes?" yelled out the captain.

"Ah, captain, I apologize. I did not know that the civilian liaison was busy," admitted a feminine voice, who seemed amused.

"Wipe that grin off your face and tell me what you want, civilian!" yelled out Nicole so that she could hear.

"Just got word that our contracts are going to be extended because of the war. Any idea how we are going to get paid?" asked the civilian.

"The captain and I will let you know soon; for now, please be patient."

"Of course, I apologize for disturbing the both of you." And once she finished her remark, one could hear footsteps walking away from the door.

"Duty calls, ensign. Talk with the civilians and let me know if the quantum-backed crypto-credit is a feasible means of payment," ordered the captain with a grin.

"I'll get right on it, sir!" teased Nicole, and they both got dressed.

The Quantum Entanglement signal technician heard a beep, alerting him that a signal was being received. He worked in a massive room, with hundreds of signal technicians working side by side, wearing headphones. Seeing that the signal was an Admiralty signal, however non-emergency in priority, he waited for the console to print out the sealed message before taking it in hand and carrying it to one of the mail chutes. He threw the message into the chute and returned to his console.

The message was picked up by one of the Admiralty building secretaries, who stepped out of the message room in search of a supervisor. She found one and filled her in on the problem that she faced.

"Supervisor, a moment please," asked the secretary.

"Yes, secretary?" replied the supervisor.

"I have a quantum entanglement message for Admiral Hackett; however, he is no longer in the building, nor is he an admiral."

"I see; must be a naval vessel that has not yet gotten the news about the change in government. Wait here, secretary." The supervisor promptly left.

The secretary waited for several moments before the supervisor returned with orders from someone higher in the command chain.

"I'll take the message from here; thank you, secretary," said the supervisor, and she took the message from the secretary, who immediately returned to the message room.

The supervisor, with the message in hand, went straight to the Admiralty floor in search of someone with enough power to either take the message from her or clear her for a trip to the Presidential Residence. She made her way to the Admiralty floor and handed off the message to the floor's secretary, who promptly went to find the newest admiral in the building, the commodore who was Admiral Hackett's right-hand man.

She went to his office, the same office that Admiral Hackett used when he was still an admiral, and knocked on the door.

"Come on in," said the admiral upon hearing the knock.

The secretary walked in and went straight to the admiral's desk.

"A message for 'Admiral Hackett,' unknown sender, sir," said the secretary, who handed the admiral the message, still sealed in its envelope.

"Unknown sender, you say. I will make sure that this message finds its way directly into the hands of the President. Thank you, secretary."

"My pleasure, sir." And the secretary left the room.

Not having much to do, especially since the reforms that were handed down to the Navy by the President several weeks ago more or less exterminated the bickering, gossip, and petty politics that plagued the Admiralty back in the administration of President Varis, the admiral decided to pay his old friend and Commander in Chief a visit. He waited a few moments for the secretary to return to her desk before starting a call.

The secretary accepted the request almost instantly. "Yes, Admiral?"

"I don't have much to do today. As such, I plan on delivering this message personally to the President. Mind requesting clearance for a meeting?" asked the admiral.

"Gladly, sir. One moment." The secretary put the call on hold as she talked with the Presidential Residence.

"Good news, sir. The President does not have a busy schedule today; they can fit you in if you arrive at the residence in an hour's time."

"Perfect. Confirm the visit with the residence and get me a pilot and aircraft for the trip."

"Yes, sir." And the secretary terminated the call.

It took around fifteen minutes for the aircraft to arrive, and the secretary let the admiral know that his ride was ready. With the average distance by air from the Admiralty building to the Presidential Residence being roughly twenty minutes, the timing could not be better. The admiral left the Admiralty building, walked to the aircraft, and boarded it.

"Welcome aboard, Admiral," said the pilot.

"Thank you for having me. You know the destination?" asked the admiral.

"Indeed, I do, sir; we will be there momentarily."

The pilot lifted off from the Admiralty building and aimed the aircraft straight at the Presidential Residence before accelerating to full speed. The ride was quick and comfortable, and the admiral arrived at the Presidential Residence after just seventeen minutes of flying.

"I'll be waiting here to take you back, sir."

"Sounds good, pilot. I shouldn't be too long; take a break."

"Gladly, sir."

The admiral stepped out of the aircraft and entered the Presidential Residence. After being cleared by security, he entered the building and went straight to the President's office. He was stopped by one of the guards since the President was currently in a meeting. The admiral took a seat on one of the chairs in the hallway and waited for the meeting to conclude.

Once the meeting concluded, he was allowed to enter by the Presidential guard, and he did so without wasting any time.

"The admiral's bar suit suits you well, my old friend," remarked the President with a smile as the admiral walked up to him and shook his hand.

"Thank you, sir; the standard issue politician suit and tie look good on you as well," replied the admiral with a grin.

"Don't you start. Anyway, what brings you to my humble office?" asked the President as he made his way back to the Presidential chair.

"A message, sir, addressed to 'Admiral Hackett,' unknown sender. It was received by the quantum entanglement signal technicians back at the Admiralty building. Since I do not have all that much to do today, I thought that you would appreciate it if I delivered it to you personally."

"I certainly appreciate it; hand it over. I'm curious as to what is inside."

The admiral handed the envelope over to the President, who wasted no time in opening the message and reading its contents. It said:

"*This is the Shiny Room reporting to Admiral Hackett. The main mission objective still eludes us; we are, however, currently in pursuit of a strong lead. Solar Empire activity in the deep systems has declined drastically over the past few months. We do not know how the war is going, but enemy forces seem to be running thin behind their lines.*"

"*The lead in question was detected in the seventh terraformed system that we visited. The seventh objective was untouched by the Solar Empire. We landed an expedition and recovered several biological samples; we are currently testing them to see if they hide any further clues and leads that may help us locate the Terraforming Installation. The lead was contained in the form of a transmitter, broadcasting an old dialect of our language that has not been used since the days of the Human Unity.*"

"*The lead instructed us to find a specific nomad ship, the Jalalight. Its location is supposedly in the outermost reaches of the Perseus arm, deep in the frontier. Since seven solar systems have not resulted in any developments, and investigation into the transmitter appears to corroborate its Human Unity origin, we have decided to investigate the lead fully by traveling to the outermost reaches of the Perseus arm in search of the Jalalight, as well as stopping by the two terraformed systems that are en route to the outer reaches of the Perseus arm. That is all, Admiral. Good luck and fortune in the war effort.*"

The President put down the message as he finished reading.

"Well, the Shiny Room is still alive and kicking."

"That is good news, Mr. President!"

"Perhaps. Do you mind staying for a while longer, Admiral? I am going to summon the Admiralty and Generalcy for a war meeting, and even though you are the newest member among the Admiralty, I would like you to participate and lend us your expertise and opinion."

"You are the President, sir; you order, I obey."

"That's a good man. In the meantime, get yourself some lunch; the culinary team in my residence is exemplary."

"With pleasure, Mr. President."

Chapter Twelve

The President remained seated at the conference table as the respective admirals and generals walked in and sat in their pre-assigned seats. It took a few moments, but eventually, everyone was seated, and the war meeting could begin.

"Thank you, everyone, for arriving on such short notice. I have just been given, as of an hour ago, intelligence that is vital for the eventual supremacy of our civilization in our galaxy. I do not believe the entirety of the admirals and generals has been briefed regarding this matter, and if you have, not to the level that I would like. Hence, this meeting is first and foremost to get everyone on the same page; secondly, to enact a strategy that I have just come up with. Colonel, begin the presentation," ordered the President.

"Yes, Mr. President. First and foremost, the history of this matter. Several years ago, several admirals, including the then Admiral Hackett, began to receive vague intelligence about the possible existence of a terraforming installation. Among the Republic, these things are more myth and legend than anything that can be verified as legitimate; however, the intelligence reports were credible enough to merit pursuing."

"We immediately ran into roadblocks placed by the Varis administration, which was concerned about the possibility of angering the Solar Empire since the reports all mentioned that the possible sightings of the terraforming installation were within Solar Empire space. Thankfully, the clandestine military buildup that many of us have secretly pursued for the last decade allowed us to allocate some intelligence resources toward pursuing these leads, culminating with the interception of a crucial dossier."

"This dossier listed dozens of terraformed systems that were discovered by the Solar Empire. The Solar Empire also strongly believed, through additional evidence and the fact that the terraformed worlds in these systems were more or less mirror copies of Earth, that the terraforming installation was an object that was real and spent significant time and resources trying to locate it."

"Before the beginning of this war, then Admiral Hackett clandestinely took the Shiny Moon out of mothballs. It was an aging cruiser, small enough that her departure would not raise suspicions among the Varis administration, but large enough to have a fighting chance at accomplishing the mission. Furthermore, the commanding officer, Captain William Nagy, is a heavily decorated sailor who served valiantly as captain of the Shiny Moon during many of the frontier engagements with the Solar Empire and various pirate organizations before the 89th was mothballed and turned into a reserve fleet."

"Let us not forget he was wise in terms of keeping morale up among his sailors. A thousand prostitutes aboard a single ship? Lucky bastards," interrupted one of the admirals, and the room laughed at the remark.

"What can I say? William was always a wildcard. Anyway, please continue, Colonel," ordered the President.

"Yes, Mr. President. The Shiny Moon so far has done well. She confirmed the existence of both the terraformed worlds as well as the Terraforming Installation. This discovery prompted many among the military to finally act against the Solar Empire and inflict a brutal first attack against our rival foe. This attack allowed us to destroy tens of thousands of her ships while they still slept in their shipyard worlds and weakened the Solar Empire enough to allow not only for the activation of our mothballed forces but also to keep the military buildup a secret until we dealt with the Varis administration. Finally, the President wishes to amend the current war strategy; that is why he called all of you to this meeting," finished the Colonel.

"Thank you, Colonel. As he said, I indeed wish to amend the war strategy. Before I begin, however, how go the latest reports from the front?" asked the President.

"Well, sir, the enemy fleets have been routed, and we are beginning to flood their borders with our own forces. Assuming they do not pull any surprises on us, which is unlikely considering the thrashing we gave them right at the start of the war with the sneak attack, I believe we will have the entirety of the Solar Empire subjugated and conquered within two to three months," replied one of the generals, and the entire room began to clap and cheer briefly; his words were what the Republic of Earth military wanted to hear for hundreds of years.

"Excellent news. In that case, my amendment to the military strategy will fit in perfectly. The Shiny Moon, in their most recent message to me, said that a nomad ship by the name of Jalalight has the location of the Terraforming Installation. The lead tells them that the ship is somewhere in the very distant end of the Perseus arm. In light of this information, I want a significant military detachment from our main fighting force to split off and head straight to the end of the arm. I want it to be small yet sizable, a fleet of a hundred or so of our newest ships constructed clandestinely over the past decade, enough to humble any pirate or nomad force."

"A wise move, but I question the size of the force, sir," said one of the admirals.

"Are a hundred ships insufficient?" replied the President.

"Indeed. Did the Shiny Moon specify the specific region of the Perseus arm, other than the far end, where this nomad ship may be located?" asked the admiral.

"Negative. The only specific part in the message was that the lead mentioned the name of the ship and the general location. Anywhere in the far end of the Perseus arm is fair game," replied the President.

"Just as I suspected. In that case, we are going to need a massive force, not only to pacify and garrison the entirety of the Perseus arm—something I strongly recommend once news about the fall of the Solar Empire begins to spread across the galaxy—but to methodically comb the end of the arm for this ship," suggested the admiral.

"I agree with you, Admiral. In that case, I am going to have to scrap a good majority of my plan. How do you see the invasion and then the pacification of the Perseus arm unfolding?" asked the President.

"Truthfully, Mr. President? I am as bewildered as you are," replied the admiral.

"No worries, that is why we are all here. Any other suggestions?" asked the President, and many palms went up. The President smiled and selected one at random, and he wasted no time in sharing his view on the matter.

The Shiny Moon had just finished her survey of the first of the two systems that lay on the path toward the end of the Perseus arm. The more or less same result was had for this system compared to all of the others. The only main difference was the layout of the terraformed planets; each planet had a unique sea, continent, and ocean layout.

"Captain, mind meeting me in my office?" asked the head doctor.

"Certainly, I'll be right down," replied the captain without delay.

Once the Shiny Moon entered FTL, the captain gave control of the bridge to his first officer and made his way to the elevator, riding it down to the medical deck. Once he arrived, he walked the deck toward the head doctor's office. He was happy to see that most of the medical staff were idle, thanks to the high level of health among his crew.

Reaching the door that led to the head doctor's office, the captain knocked four times, then paused, awaiting a response.

"Yes?" said a voice, unmistakably that of the head doctor.

"It's the captain; you summoned me?"

"Ah yes, please come in, sir."

The captain opened the bulkhead door and entered the office. It was filled with papers, all neatly stacked and facing the door; clearly, the doctor prepared them to be reviewed by someone.

"Judging by all of these papers, you have some news regarding the biological samples that we recovered on the seventh terraformed world?" asked the captain, who sat down in front of the desk and began to peruse.

"That is correct, sir."

"Interesting; your team did not hold back."

"No, they didn't, sir; as you can see for yourself, the lifeforms that we encountered have an unmistakable lineage to life found on Earth. The DNA is just too similar to justify an independent evolution of life."

The papers strongly corroborated the aforementioned origins of life on the seventh terraformed planet. Compared to the equivalent species of Earth origin, the DNA was around 94% similar, with several additions that seemed to be direct edits in the DNA code. All strong evidence of the controller AI modifying life for terraforming alien worlds, as well as further evidence for the existence of the Terraforming Installation itself.

"Did you find anything fancy in the DNA, doctor?"

"Fancy, in what way, sir?"

"In the way that can help us find the Terraforming Installation that seeded this life on the world that we took it from," replied the captain.

"Nothing that meets that definition, unfortunately."

"That's fine; the material that we have here is excellent."

The captain continued to peruse the different papers. Much of the data he could not understand, but of the material that he did understand, it was enough to get a rough picture. Some DNA was added to different organisms directly; the specific code could be found in the same sequence on other organisms that share no close lineage. This gave interesting traits.

For one, the bird carcass that was recovered contained interesting genetic traits that were not found in any other bird that lived on Earth. The most notable trait was the addition of cellulose to the cytoskeleton, allowing some of the tissues to be rigid whenever necessary, for example, during impact against a solid surface at high speed. Ripper rounds, of course, shredded the intricate structure without any problem.

"I'm still trying to picture how long," Captain Nagy said out loud.

"How long what, sir?" asked the head doctor.

"How long it took the Terraforming Installation to both terraform and seed that seventh world that we visited with life," replied the captain.

"That's a good question; maybe it started the process and left?"

"If that is the case, why didn't we find any terraforming technology?"

"Good point, sir."

The captain and the head doctor continued to talk for about an hour before the meeting was concluded. The captain went back to the bridge, resumed command until the start of the night shift, then retired to his quarters for the night. He repeated the process again and again, with rare interruptions, for several months until the Shiny Moon arrived at the far end of the Perseus arm.

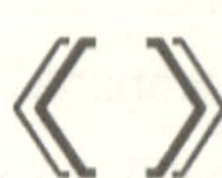

The first officer had taken over from the night shift several hours previously. The Shiny Moon was navigating uncharted space, searching for any signs of human activity or settlement. Today was her lucky day.

"Sir, I think we have something," said the head sensor officer through the communication line.

"What kind of signal?" asked the first officer.

"Radio wave, FM modulated frequency. Too scrambled for any data to be extracted from it, but too precise and repeated for it to be a natural occurrence. My guess is it's a signal that was distorted through a nebula."

"Direction?"

"About 17 degrees southwest of our current bow."

"Helm, anything interesting in that heading?"

"Negative, First Officer, not for at least eighty or so light years."

The first officer sighed. Such a distance means that whoever transmitted this signal originally did so roughly a century ago. He hesitated for a moment before responding.

"Alright, sensor team, I want that signal deciphered. The actual contents are no doubt too corroded and distorted to give us the data that it was originally transmitting, but information that could tell us if it was a ship or planet, as well as specific distortions through atmosphere or gases, I want to know about it," ordered the first officer.

"We'll get right on it, sir," replied the head sensor officer.

"Helmsman, change course, 17 degrees southwest of current bow."

"Changing, sir," replied the helmsman.

Captain Nagy woke up and repeated the same routine he had been following for over five months. He prepared himself, got dressed, and left his quarters. The crew did not even blink as they saw him walking from his quarters to his chair. The first officer smiled at the sight of his old friend.

"Bridge is yours, sir," said the first officer.

"Thank you, First Officer. Anything new since I lost consciousness?" asked the captain with an early morning smile.

"Yes, our sensor team just picked up a heavily distorted signal. Radio wave, FM modulated frequency. Very unlikely that we will be able to get data from it, but I had the team get started on analyzing what exactly distorted the signal. I had the helm change heading to the source of the signal, 17 degrees southwest of bow. Nothing interesting there for around eighty light years," replied the first officer, summarizing everything that had just recently occurred.

"Very well, we will proceed without any changes then."

"Captain," asked the helmsman.

"Yes?"

"How was your sleep?"

"It was good, helmsman. Thank you for asking. Now keep flying."

"With pleasure, sir."

The Shiny Moon continued on its course for a few days until the sensor team began to detect a massive amount of radio signals.

"Helmsman, drop us out of FTL. Full stop," ordered the captain.

"Dropping. Full stop, captain," replied the helmsman.

"Well, head sensor officer, what is it?" asked the captain.

"A cornucopia of signals, sir; I reckon that it is a sizeable human settlement that communicates with each other primarily through radio. Signals are intact enough to transcribe; give us a few to find out what we are dealing with," replied the head sensor officer in an excited voice.

"Gladly, it's not like we have anything better to do." The captain's remark elicited some laughter from the bridge crew.

Ten minutes passed before the head sensor officer spoke again.

"Definitely a large space station or planetary settlement. Lots of 'entertainment' signals, comedic shows, and other podcast-like material, all broadcast through radio waves," relayed the head sensor officer.

"Somewhat foolish of them to broadcast using radio?" remarked the first officer.

"Where are the signals coming from?" asked the captain.

"78 degrees east of our current course," replied the head sensor officer.

"Anything interesting in that direction?" asked the captain.

"There is a cluster of stars; we can reach them in a few days at FTL," replied the helmsman.

"Set course for them."

"Right away, sir."

The Solar Empire had more or less crumbled by this point in the war, and President Hackett was being inundated with diplomatic requests from all four corners of the galaxy as word about the great defeat spread.

"Alright, list me the three largest and/or most powerful nations that request a meeting with me," ordered President Hackett.

"The Nebula Kingdom. The Rock Syndicate. Qutalin," replied the presidential staffer.

"Qutalin? Who the hell are they?"

"A religious civilization; they own a wide stretch of land beyond The Rock Syndicate. They descended from religious settlers who settled what was then the frontier of humanity back in the days of the Human Unity."

"I see. I will speak with their ambassador first. Send him in."

President Hackett did not need to wait long. Just a few minutes after the presidential staffer left the office, the ambassador for Qutalin walked in and bowed in deep respect to the president. President Hackett was pleased at the sight.

"Thank you, ambassador, for arriving on such short notice."

"Thank you for honoring me with an acceptance of my request."

"Of course, Ambassador; please take a seat and tell me what is on your mind," said President Hackett, who motioned for the ambassador to take a seat in front of his desk. The ambassador promptly obeyed.

"With pleasure, Mr. President. I first have to congratulate you on your rise to power and on your incredible victory against the now-destroyed Solar Empire. For decades, they have been a nuisance to our trade; all of Qutalin was very happy indeed when we heard of their demise."

"As am I, Ambassador. A joyous day for our two great nations."

"Indeed, Mr. President," replied the ambassador with a smile.

"I apologize for my ignorance, but I have not heard much about your nation. I know that you lie beyond the Rock Syndicate; I assume you have a strong relationship with them?" asked President Hackett.

"You are correct on both counts, sir."

"I see. Well, in that case, I ask that we delve straight into the topic that brought you here today. What interests do the Qutalin have?"

"Trade and non-aggression, Mr. President. Since you are now the largest and no doubt most powerful nation in the local region, we want to help add to your economy through mutual trade. In pursuit of such an ambition, we wish to immediately enter into a non-aggression pact with you."

"Two reasonable ambitions. Your request for a non-aggression pact is granted. Have the terms drafted, and I will send them to our legislature for ratification. Regarding trade, that is a topic that is vast and will likely take several days to discuss. I ask that you wait for two or more weeks on that matter; we still need to catalog all our new acquisitions."

"I have no issues with that. Thank you, Mr. President, for your time and wise decisions!" said the ambassador as he left the presidential office after shaking President Hackett's hand.

The presidential staffer came rushing in once the ambassador left.

"Welcome back, staffer. Bring in the ambassador from the Nebula Kingdom, followed by the one from the Rock Syndicate," ordered President Hackett.

"Right away, Mr. President," replied the presidential staffer before leaving.

Two hours passed, and President Hackett had met with over ten different ambassadors. A dozen more were waiting to be summoned by him, and more continued to arrive. The president was done with diplomacy for the day. He picked up his phone and called his main secretary. She picked up immediately without any delay.

"Yes, Mr. President?"

"I'm done with the ambassadors for today. Tell them to retire for the day. If I do not get to them by tomorrow, start having the diplomatic corps talk and negotiate with them."

"I'll let them know right away, sir."

Somewhat hungry, the president decided to have lunch. As he walked the halls toward the residence kitchen, the president could not get out of his mind the hilariously ironic statement that he had said to each and every ambassador he spoke with today: 'Draft the terms, and I will send them to our legislature for ratification.' The fact that the legislature, for the most part, was liquidated on his orders after they refused to accept his legitimacy was hilarious to him. The legislature existed to do whatever he wanted, after all.

Chapter Thirteen

"Captain, we are coming up on the origin system of all our radio waves," barked the helmsman, snapping Captain Nagy out of the daydream trance he escapes to during periods of inactivity.

"Excellent, drop us out of warp at the system's edge, standard first contact protocol with another nation," ordered the captain.

"Yes, sir," replied the helmsman.

The Shiny Moon dropped out of FTL warp, and as the warpers cooled down, she began to analyze every single signal she could pick up. Hundreds of different vessels were all leaving and approaching a terrestrial world near the edge of the inner solar system.

"Captain, we have a signal being sent directly to us from the planet. It is very strong and was just recently created," said the head sensor officer through the wire.

"It's more than likely their greeting. Decode, translate it, and send it to the bridge," ordered the captain.

"Will do, sir," replied the head sensor officer.

"Unknown vessel, please state the flag you fly under and your purpose here." The message continued to repeat over and over.

"Unknown planet, this is the Republic of Earth Cruiser Shiny Moon. We only harbor peaceful intentions; may we ask the flag you fly under?" replied the Shiny Moon, the computer having no issue communicating and translating in their specific nomadic dialect.

"We fly under no flag; we are all free men here," replied the planet.

"I see. We request permission to orbit and possibly land if you have a torch-engine-resistant spaceport," asked the Shiny Moon.

"We do have a torch-engine-resistant spaceport. For now, you are permitted to orbit while we get a better look at you. Approach slowly with torch engines only," replied the planet.

"We shall do as you say. Thank you," said the Shiny Moon.

"A planet of free men; I've never seen such a sight," marveled the first officer.

"There is no way they could survive closer to human civilization. Out here, however, one can be free with plenty of warning," replied the captain.

"Indeed, sir. Still an astonishing sight."

"Agreed, first officer. Helmsman, do as the nomads request."

"Right away, captain."

The Shiny Moon slowly approached the planet and entered into an elliptical orbit at a decent distance of several hundred miles from the planetary surface. Several ships approached and scanned the Shiny Moon before she got close, then peeled away. They remained at a distance, but still close enough to engage in combat if the situation demanded it.

"Shiny Moon, we have never seen a ship from the Republic of Earth all the way out here. What brings you to our humble planet? Especially a ship that has passed her best years?" asked the planet.

"Searching for answers," replied the Shiny Moon.

"I see, Shiny Moon. To what questions?"

"There is a specific vessel that has information that could be valuable to us. We only know her by her name, the Jalalight. Any chance that you know of her?"

"Jalalight, you say? Very interesting. We do know of her; however, she has never visited our world. The ship that you seek is massive; she lives among the stars, sustained by tribute paid to her by those who seek knowledge."

"Seekers of knowledge? Are they information brokers?"

"In a way, yes. They are crewed by a nation that adores new sights and experiences. They trade knowledge for new knowledge."

"I see. Do you know where we can find her?"

"Possibly, but like all things deep in the frontier, such knowledge has a price. Our economy does not get many new travelers. Do you bring anything that could be of interest to us?"

The captain thought for a moment before smiling. "Yes, nomad world, we have some old laser weaponry that we did not have time to repair. If you help us remove it from our hull, the turrets are yours to do with as you wish. The supplementary power and targeting systems, however, we need to keep."

"No worries, Shiny Moon. Those turrets by themselves could be repurposed into powerful mining lasers. I think that we can both help each other very nicely. Our spaceport is on one side of a mountain range; it serves well as a torch engine exhaust shield. We will send you coordinates for approach and landing. We'll send a greeting party over to you once you land."

"Understood, thank you for having us."

"Our pleasure, enjoy your stay!"

The captain smiled as he asked out loud, "It isn't paradise, but the atmosphere seems breathable enough. Why not stay for some shore leave before setting off once more into the void?"

"No one aboard this tin can will say no to that, sir, but I strongly suggest we wait until we get more information about the planet and her people before allowing the crew to disembark," replied the first officer.

"Agreed, we'll revisit this topic at a later time. For now, prepare the ship for landing," ordered the captain, and everyone immediately got to work.

"All hands, all hands, please man your landing stations. All hands, all hands, please man your landing stations," said the bosun, and the command echoed throughout the ship, thanks to the loudspeakers.

The nomad planet did not take long to send over the landing coordinates and instructions. A specific entry point was given by which the Shiny Moon was to enter, then decelerate using her torch engines as she slowly landed. The thrust was to be as light as possible, enough to slow the vessel down to a full stop. The mountains would shield the settlement on the other side from the superheated plasma exhaust.

"Alright, all hands ready?" asked the captain.

"All hands ready, sir," replied the bosun.

"Helmsman, give me magic," ordered the captain.

"Right away, sir!" replied the helmsman.

The ship turned around just as the burn window opened and started to run her torch drives at minimum thrust. Her speed rapidly decreased until the velocity was low enough for the planet's gravity to start pulling the ship toward the surface. The ship began to dip and enter the atmosphere, on the exact course that was outlined by the nomad planet.

"Increasing thrust gradient, 0.1% increase per second until 2% of total capacity," said the helmsman.

"Noted. Hold at 2% total capacity until we need to kill velocity right before landing; once there, increase to 3%," ordered the captain.

"Roger that, sir."

The ship slowed down and scattered in front of her a great plume of plasma as she punched through the atmosphere. The ambient temperature of the landing valley began to increase, and as the ship got closer and closer, the sandy dust began to darken, then char, and finally turn into glass as the heat intensified. The entire valley was filled with such scars, especially as one got closer to the mountain range, a result of thousands of torch engine landings over the years.

"Approaching the landing pad, increasing thrust to 3%."

The Shiny Moon stabilized at 3%, and she landed on her landing legs gently and without any issues. The entire landing pad, as well as the surrounding area, glowed red with heat. The pad, however, remained stable and firm under the ship's weight.

"Ship landed, sir, and the foundation appears perfectly stable."

"Thank you, helmsman. Excellent work on the landing. Now to wait until the land around us cools down," said the captain with a smile.

"I don't believe that waiting until it cools down will be necessary. We have several aircraft approaching us, captain," replied the head sensor officer.

The aircraft rapidly approached the Shiny Moon, and once they were in range, began to pour water both onto and all around the ship. A great cloud of steam formed, and the remnant water boiled as it absorbed the heat from the surrounding ground. The aircraft, however, came prepared with a significant amount of water, and they continued to pour all around the ship, generating more and more steam, until the temperature cooled down enough that no more steam could be seen.

The remnant water was dumped onto the Shiny Moon, helping to cool her off even further, as well as all around the ship, turning the surrounding area into muddy muck. Once the temperature was safe for landing and traversing, the water-carrying aircraft left, leaving behind a single aircraft that landed near the ship.

"First officer, you have the bridge; I'm going to meet our hosts."

"Understood, captain. Good luck."

"Head sensor officer, is the atmosphere breathable?" asked the captain as he walked toward the elevator, slowing down as he waited for a response from the head sensor officer.

"Barely, sir; I'd take an oxygen mask with you."

"Will do, thank you, head sensor officer."

The captain left the bridge without any further delay; he entered the elevator and went straight down to the ground floor of the ship. The deck compartments had already rotated into place as per surface protocol, and the gravity deck plates had turned off. The gravity felt somewhat different; the world was likely a little less than 1g. It was a good feeling; it made you feel slightly stronger than you actually are.

The elevator reached the ground floor, and the captain stepped out. He walked the deck until he reached the door to the outside and then turned left until he found a small medical storage room. Next to the first aid kits and other medical supplies were small oxygen tanks with plastic masks. The captain picked one up, fastened the tank to his belt, and put the mask on, making sure that the plastic tube wrapped comfortably around his waist before hugging his back and then left shoulder as it arrived at his face.

Twisting the nozzle until he felt a slight breeze of gas on his face, the captain proceeded to walk back toward the airlock door and entered the airlock chamber. He saw a group of nomads waiting patiently around the ship, staring at the landing legs and ship engines as they waited. The captain opened the final airlock door leading outside, and he stepped onto the small balcony that had deployed once the ship finished landing.

Pressing a button, a walkable staircase rapidly unfolded until it smacked into the ground, locking itself in place once it did so. The captain walked down the staircase, and the nomads rapidly converged at the base to greet him. They all wore plastic oxygen masks, the same as the captain.

"Judging by your uniform, you must be the captain. I thank you for being the one to greet us," said one of the nomads, who extended his hand for a handshake. The captain reciprocated in kind.

The dialect spoken by the nomads was somewhat difficult to understand, thanks to centuries of vocabulary and pronunciation shifts, but it was close enough to Earthian that Captain Nagy could speak for mutual intelligibility between the speakers. These nomads were no doubt descendants of Human Unity immigrants who had arrived in this sector of the galaxy, what was then the far frontier wilderness centuries ago.

"Of course, it would be rude to send someone down and then have said person relay back to me. This way we can talk, and if we need to come to terms on something, we can do so immediately," replied the captain.

"Well, first and foremost, I am the elected mayor of the town just beyond this mountain range. A pleasure to meet you."

"Likewise, mayor; naturally, I'm sure you know why we are here."

"I was briefed on the matter as we flew over. You are searching for the Jalalight. In exchange, you offered to give us your offline laser turrets if I understand correctly?"

"You are well informed; everything you said is correct," said the captain, his smile barely visible under the plastic oxygen mask.

"Perfect, well, in that case, we can get started. I have to warn you, however, that the process is going to take time, even with the assistance of your engineers."

"We've been on this mission for the larger part of a year; we can deal with some slight delays, mayor," replied the captain, who motioned for the mayor and his entourage to follow him as he walked to one of the landing legs.

"Perfect, in that case, you have a deal. The Jalalight tends to be tricky to find, so we'll need a day or so to get the approximate location and have our cartographers talk with your navigation team and be briefed on the matter."

"No worries, mayor. Actually, now that I have you here, I would like to ask two questions of you, if you do not mind them."

"I do not mind them, captain; ask away."

"The first question is about your government structure. I apologize if the answer is dead obvious, but the Republic of Earth does not meet all that many nomads in our sector of the galaxy."

"Each settlement elects a mayor to represent them in times of necessity every year; this moment is a perfect example. All of the mayors, every five years, get together and elect a planetary governor for a term of five years. He speaks for all of us to a limited extent," replied the mayor.

"I see, and the hundreds of ships that we saw approach and leave your world, I reckon that they land next to different settlements in different areas of the planet?"

"That is correct, Captain. You were told to land here because we are a mining operation, and your laser turrets are a dream come true for us."

"I see, and secondly, is your planet part of a larger nation, or are you independent?"

"Not only are we independent, Captain, but each settlement here is independent; in fact, each man is his own nation, and each woman her own nation. I only enjoy the level of authority that my settlement gives me. If a majority wish to see my honorary position of mayor stripped from my hands, it is stripped without any further questions," replied the mayor.

"Fascinating," said the captain aloud.

The captain and the mayor talked for a few more minutes before the two parted ways. The engineering teams will be arriving in an hour's time, and the captain and the mayor agreed to talk again once they arrive, in pursuit of even more potential agreements, such as shore leave for the crew and other additional trades of goods and services once the question of the nomads possibly accepting Earth Quantum-Backed Crypto-Credits is addressed.

Returning to the bridge, with the oxygen tank and mask still attached at his side, the captain sat back down in his chair.

"We have ourselves a deal. We help them remove the laser turrets; they give us as close to a definitive location regarding the Jalalight as possible. Apparently, they do not like being found all that easily. Furthermore, the topic of shore leave did come up. Once we resolve the little dispute regarding currency, I think that we can approve shore leave for the entire crew," said the captain.

"Very nice work, sir," replied the bosun.

"I always do good work, bosun. Thank you for the kind words, however."

"While security procedures would stress the necessity of doing thorough research on these people, the very fact that we landed on their world in the first place somewhat removes such considerations from the mind. After all, if they wish us harm, there is not much that we can do about it," added the first officer.

"Correction, First Officer; I can overload our reactor in such a way that this planet would be uninhabitable for several decades. If they wish us dead, they will get their wish, but the price will be steep," added the head engineer, who spoke through a communications line.

"Really, how would you go about doing that?" asked the captain.

"It's quite simple, Captain; you need a certain element called cobalt, specifically the isotope Cobalt-60. You need a lot of it, which can be done if I program the reactor in such a way to ensure as much of it is produced from the elements onboard as possible. I make enough of a blast, and this planet is going to be a pain in the ass to live under for quite some time," replied the head engineer, who enjoyed discussing one of his many theoretical concepts.

"Frankly, sir, these people do not have much in the way of industry; our laser turrets themselves will jumpstart their mining, industrial, and scientific capabilities by decades. Something else is puzzling to me: the radio waves that we detected, which led us to this planet. They betray the fact that humans have lived on this planet for well over a hundred years. Why still so stagnant in development?" asked the helmsman, wanting to join in on the conversation with his own philosophical dilemma.

"From speaking to them, I think they really do not care all that much about working to build up a civilization as we know it. Their world, slowly but surely, is being terraformed, and they are happy. They get lots of trade from other nomad ships, and now they have a lucky ship that brings forth bountiful goodies and new people to meet. It is a simple life, which brings them a special reward of its own," replied the captain.

"Well said, Captain; that more or less solves my dilemma perfectly," added the helmsman, satisfied with Captain Nagy's answer.

The bridge crew of the Shiny Moon waited for over one hour until the first of the nomad engineering teams started to arrive via aircraft. The respective aerial vehicles landed all around the ship, and the engineering teams began to unload several tools that would be needed for the salvage job.

Chapter Fourteen

"Alright, time to go and speak with the mayor. Hopefully, he brings good news regarding the currency situation. Any concerns or important pieces of information that you would like me to relay to the mayor and his people?" asked the captain.

"There is one thing, captain. Tell them that the laser turrets are safe to begin disassembling; after all, power has not flowed through their circuit veins in over a decade. We have juiced them up just enough so that they can be rotated; they are facing directly broadside and should be a breeze to remove once the necessary elbow grease is applied. Furthermore, tell them that the ship engineers would be happy to assist if needed," replied the head engineer.

"Understood, head engineer. Anyone else?"

"Tell them that quantum-backed crypto-credits are impossible to forge and will always be worth something!" said the bosun pleadingly.

"Understood, bosun. Don't worry; I think they will understand. Very well, bridge, I will see everyone later. First officer, the ship is yours."

"Understood, sir. Happy travels," replied the first officer.

The captain got up from his chair, rode the elevator down to the ground deck, and exited the ship through the same airlock that he had used previously. Walking down the staircase connected to the airlock, the captain could see the mayor of the nearby nomad settlement waiting for him.

"Once again, a pleasure, mayor," said the captain out loud.

"The pleasure is mine, captain. Fortunately, I believe that I have some good news regarding the dilemma of currency that we briefly covered in our previous conversation," replied the mayor.

"I'm all ears, mayor."

"One of the settlements on our world specializes in computers and advanced communication systems. I have put in a special request, and they have confirmed the existence of your 'quantum-backed crypto-credit' currency. Apparently, it is quite common for ships that patrol the frontier; after all, it is easier to pay the sailors using such technology."

"That's why the admiralty does it. Nothing beats a physical credit chip; however, it's a more personal form of money, and it's easier to accept."

"Indeed, however, back to the matter at hand. They are flying over several computer technicians with quantum readers; they will charge us a small fee and convert your money into several local currencies that are used in this sector of space. This allows us to accept your currency without any issues!" said the mayor eagerly.

"Excellent, in that case, I'll authorize shore leave for my crew. Will shuttling them to and from your settlement be a problem?"

"Negative, Captain; considering the potential earnings from customers with deep pockets who could not spend their hard-earned money aboard your vessel, we will gladly shuttle them to and from their ship as often as they would like."

"Perfect. You are definitely correct about their inability to spend their hard-earned money; you'll soon see why," said Captain Nagy with an enormous grin, which was more or less obscured by the plastic oxygen mask.

The captain and the mayor continued to talk for some time before parting ways. Once the conversation was finished, the mayor gave Captain Nagy a communicator and added his respective device contact number to the contacts list. If the captain had any issues or concerns, the mayor instructed him that he was free to contact him directly at any time throughout his stay on the planet.

With the pending issues now settled, the captain returned to the ship and went to the nearest intra-ship communications panel, dialing the bridge with his personal authorization code. The computer cleared him immediately, and the bosun answered his call without delay.

"Yes, Captain?" answered the bosun, who saw the identity of the caller on his console.

"Contact the civilian liaison, as well as the head officers of the respective departments aboard the ship, and tell them that the captain requests a meeting in thirty minutes' time. Have them report to the briefing room," replied the captain clearly and with a brisk pace.

"Will do, sir."

"That is all, bosun. Thank you."

After disconnecting the call, the captain stepped away from the communications panel and made his way to the ship's galley. There, he got something to eat, both to alleviate his growing sense of hunger and to burn the thirty minutes of time before the start of the meeting. He ate his lunch in fifteen minutes, spending the other fifteen minutes walking the ship and taking in the view before reporting to the briefing room.

The briefing room had all the head officers of the different departments: head engineer, head doctor, head sensor officer, and head gunnery officer. Finally, the civilian liaison was present, with a grin appearing on her face the moment the captain entered the room.

"Perfect, everyone is here. Might as well start now; it shouldn't take all that long," the captain began the meeting with a casual tone.

"One question, sir," asked the civilian liaison.

"Ask it, ensign," replied the captain.

"Why not have this meeting through communicators instead of in person? It seems so corporate to me."

"The answer to that question is quite simple, ensign. It is standard naval protocol and procedure. I understand that we are bending the protocols to a massive degree on this mission, but there are certain protocols that exist for a reason. A meeting between officers that is done in person is one of them."

"Improved sense of camaraderie?"

"In a way. Naval life can be monotonous and boring; forcing the officers of the crew to interact has many benefits. Finally, I prefer having the meeting in person, and since I am the highest-ranking officer, this means that meetings aboard this ship are done in person."

"Understood, sir."

"Returning to the topic of this meeting, I've spoken with the mayor, and he has cleared the use of our quantum-backed crypto-credits. One of the other settlements that specializes in technology and computers is able to accept the currency. They will be flying over to act as exchange brokers for the settlement, taking a small fee in order to convert our credit currency into local currency used around this sector of space. This naturally means that shore leave is possible, and considering the current situation, where our crew has not felt the touch of a planetary surface in over six months, it is arguably necessary for the maintenance of our crew's morale. I want to develop a set schedule for departures and arrivals; the nomads will be shuttling us to and from the ship, but I do not want this to become a chaotic mess like those cheap interstellar cruises whenever they land on a new world," concluded the captain.

It took about twenty minutes, but the meeting ended up being fruitful. A logical and organized list of shore leave was developed, with a mixture of participants from all the different ship departments in each group. The groups alternate, allowing for at least two shore leave visits to the nearby nomad settlement each day. It will have to be modified as the days go by until the end of the shore leave, but it was a good enough system to start. The shore leave for the crew will start tomorrow, a reasonable enough time to allow for the computer technicians with quantum readers from the other nomad settlement to arrive.

With a plan set and ready for implementation starting tomorrow, the captain concluded the meeting, and everyone went off to return to their respective duties. Now alone in the briefing room, the captain thought about the quantum-backed crypto-credits, and suddenly, a wild idea hit him like a brick thrown at maximum force. He pulled out the communicator that the mayor had given him and made a call to the sole contact stored on the device. The mayor picked it up after only a few seconds of ringing.

"So soon, captain!" joked the mayor with a laugh.

"Indeed, I apologize, but a wild idea just hit me," replied the captain.

"Do tell, captain."

"You mentioned that the computer technicians who are arriving to facilitate the exchange of our quantum-backed currency are from another settlement, no?" asked the captain with glee in his voice.

"That is correct, captain," replied the mayor with a tone of curiosity.

"In addition, you mentioned that this settlement specializes in technology and computers. Is it safe to assume that each settlement on this world specializes in something? You mentioned mining for yours, and now this other settlement has computers and other technology as a specialty."

"Still correct, captain."

"Mind listing all of the other settlements on this world and the respective skills and specialties that they command?"

"Planning on making a large purchase?" said the mayor with a laugh.

"That exact thing is a potential possibility," replied the captain.

The mayor listed off the settlements from memory and the respective trade that the majority of the population tends to specialize in. The captain could not help but smile as the mayor continued to speak; his wild card plan ended up being a feasible one after all.

"Perfect, Mayor, I'll be contacting you shortly with an update."

"Sounds good, Captain. Until then," the mayor ended the call.

With glee and passion, Captain Nagy got up from his chair. He raced to the sensor deck and traversed the area at record pace before entering the quantum communications room. The sailors manning the consoles, all junior-faced young ensigns straight out of the academy, rocketed out of their seats, standing at attention with a salute.

"At ease, gentlemen," said the captain, and the sailors stood at ease.

"What can we do for you, sir?" asked one of the signal technicians.

"I have an urgent message that needs to be sent directly to the Admiralty," replied the captain.

"We can handle it, sir. Priority emergency?"

"Negative, it's not that important. Send it to the Admiralty building, have the bearer be Admiral Hackett, under priority urgent."

The signal technician quickly navigated his console, and in a few moments, he was ready to transcribe and send whatever message the captain had in mind.

"Ready, sir," said the signal technician.

"Admiral Hackett, this is William Nagy speaking. We have come across a wildly unique opportunity, which we cannot exploit without your assistance. We have landed on a nomad world, a civilization most peculiar. They have no central government; the entire planet is a loosely allied confederation of settlements, which appears to have a small and decentralized government that does the bare minimum of governance whenever the need presents itself. A form of government that is not quite that far off from our own, I must say."

"After some difficulty, we have convinced them to accept our quantum-backed crypto-credits, of which we have in abundance aboard the ship, as suitable currency for commerce. They have several settlements that specialize in ship maintenance; this world is, after all, frequently visited by nomadic vessels from all across the sector. As such, I request a large sum of money be wired directly to our ship's treasury for use in retrofitting our vessel; she is in dire need of an overhaul after a decade of neglect, as I'm sure you know, Admiral."

"I request a sum of two million credits, which should be adequate to pay for an extensive retrofit and upgrade of the ship and her systems. Any remainder will be wired directly back to our government's coffers once the retrofit is complete and we depart this world. I conclude by issuing an apology. I understand this request is completely out of the ordinary, and I am certain that I am violating several regulations by requesting it, but the opportunity that has presented itself is as wild as the request, and I would be neglecting my duties as captain if I did not at least attempt to pursue it. That is all, Admiral; thank you for your time and your consideration of my request," finished the captain, who ordered the signal technician to send the message over.

After a long delay due to the size of the message, the signal technician said, "Sent, sir."

"Excellent, that will be all for today; thank you, gentlemen."

President Hackett was eating one of the best cuts of steak that he had ever had as part of an official presidential state dinner when a signal technician came racing into the room. He made his way straight to the president, who was busy eating while discussing trade treaties with three different ambassadors. He whispered something in his ear, then handed him the sealed envelope containing the quantum-transmitted message.

"Something important, Mr. President?" asked one of the ambassadors.

"Yes, but it can wait for a few minutes; I'm going to guzzle this steak down and speed up our talks for today, however," replied President Hackett, placing the envelope in his left shirt pocket.

"Fair enough, sir. In that case, I will illustrate the full portrait of concessions that The Rock Syndicate is willing to make while you enjoy your dinner. We are prepared to offer The Republic of Earth a mutual trade agreement for all goods, carried by neutral vessels of either side, subject only to a 10% tariff. This tariff applies to both parties; The Republic of Earth will, of course, be entitled to levy a tariff on all incoming trade that enters her borders," said the ambassador to The Rock Syndicate with a smile.

The mouth of President Hackett watered each and every time a piece of exceptional steak entered it, but even this delight was not enough to keep the President from issuing a rebuttal to the offer.

"You are very generous, ambassador," the President said, putting down his knife and fork. "But I have to ask, why not forgo the addition of tariffs altogether? Think about the inefficiency that it will cause each merchant, no matter the banner he may fly, as he has to register his cargo and wait for inspection. Clearly, the principle of supply and demand, which has served mankind well throughout thousands of years of scarcity, should be the path that we pursue."

"You are correct about the benefits of supply and demand and the free rein of the market in allocating scarce goods, Mr. President, but I must remind you that your economy and nation are industrialized at a level that far surpasses what we can bring to the agreement. Especially now that The Republic of Earth has completely and utterly conquered the entirety of the Solar Empire, your excess economic might will simply demolish any fledgling industry that we have. The tariff is meant to help alleviate the concerns of our industrialists; the money will be used to help negate some of the losses that they are bound to incur," replied the ambassador to The Rock Syndicate.

"I understand completely, Ambassador, and I certainly do not want to start our relationship by harming your industrial sector. But I also must remind you that our industrialists do not like to see the prices of their final product elevated artificially compared to what they would be in a free market. I am a man of compromise, and I ask for a 5% tariff for both parties. This allows you to slightly subsidize your industrialists and shield them from the blunt impact of our arrangement, but it also starves them enough to encourage your industrial sector to grow and become more productive. Is this reasonable?" asked President Hackett.

"Yes, Mr. President, we can accept a 5% tariff," replied the ambassador to the Rock Syndicate.

"Perfect, then I agree to these terms, Ambassador! I have a very strong feeling that our Congress and Senate will also agree. I'll be looking forward to signing the bill once it clears both chambers," said the President with a smile.

The President returned to eating his steak, and the two other ambassadors present in the meeting, the ambassador for the Nebula Kingdom and the ambassador for Qutalin, waited until the President had finished his dinner before continuing the negotiations. All four men ate silently; no one, after all, wanted to waste an exceptional steak.

The President was the first to break the silence once everyone cleared their plates: "Alright, now that our meals are finished, let us finalize our negotiations. I will start with you, Ambassador for Qutalin. What do you think about joining our trade agreement? Assuming, of course, that the Rock Syndicate does not mind."

"We do not, so long as the terms are just," replied the ambassador for the Rock Syndicate.

"Perfect! In that case, what do you think, Ambassador?" asked President Hackett, who looked at the ambassador for Qutalin.

"I'm assuming, of course, that you want to keep the same terms, which would be a 5% tariff for all parties involved?"

"That seems reasonable. What do you think?" asked President Hackett, turning to the ambassador for the Rock Syndicate.

"It is reasonable, but I would like for the tariff to be charged during each border crossing."

"Unacceptable. You know very well, ambassador, that your nation lies between the Republic of Earth and our space. You'll charge a tariff for free!" retorted the ambassador to Qutalin.

"Merchants are free to go around our space and evade the tariffs if they so choose."

"And be picked off by pirates and your privateers. I don't think that would be in our best interests."

"Insisting without evidence that we would dare to privateer your merchant ships—that is also not in your best interests either, ambassador."

Chapter Fifteen

Smiling as he saw an opportunity, President Hackett said, "Gentlemen, please, I did not invite you here to eat my food in the company of hospitality only to insult each other like a pair of hungry hyenas. This space in question, that you claim is infested with pirates and other pests, is it uninhabited?"

"For the most part, yes, and it is filled with gases from several local nebulas," replied the ambassador for The Rock Syndicate.

"In that case, The Republic of Earth can annex the unclaimed territory and garrison it with military forces; this allows us to drive out the pirates and provide an alternative route for merchants from Qutalin to our main space," suggested President Hackett.

The ambassadors cursed themselves for being so foolish. They had just given the now largest and strongest power in the sector a perfectly valid excuse to annex even more territory. All of this over a foolish squabble over 5% trade tariffs. They simply could not let that happen.

"Mr. President, we would not be comfortable with that," said the ambassador for Qutalin.

"Why not? It would open a safe trading route for you directly into our space, bypassing The Rock Syndicate for the cases where you would rather avoid dual tariffs. We will be glad to pacify and garrison the region ourselves at our expense," replied President Hackett.

"I concur with the ambassador for Qutalin; frankly, Mr. President, we are still adjusting to the new diplomatic map, which has already been radically altered at such short notice. Having you annex this space, while a perfectly legitimate move given that it is unclaimed and done in the name of empowering trade, puts us in an uncomfortable position that we would rather not be in," added the ambassador for The Rock Syndicate.

"I see; well, that leaves us at an impasse. I, however, do see a way out. We will forgo any claim to the space that would open up a new trade route that bypasses The Rock Syndicate. But in exchange, we want a trade bloc with no tariffs, not just between our three powers, but The Nebula Kingdom as well," said President Hackett, and everyone turned to the ambassador for The Nebula Kingdom.

The ambassador for the Nebula Kingdom could not hope to hold back the large smile that had appeared on his face. This was his first impression of the new President of the Republic of Earth, and he was impressed with what he saw. He cleverly played the two ambassadors like cheap flutes. In the end, he got exactly what he wanted: a large and all-encompassing trade bloc agreement, in which the four largest nations in the sector participated.

And to add insult to injury, no nation could charge tariffs. A massive win for the Republic of Earth, especially with her recently conquered territory that was ripe for economic development. The ambassador to the Nebula Kingdom just could not say no, even if he had wanted to.

"A free trade agreement with the four largest nations in the sector? Not only does the Nebula Kingdom accept, but I have no doubt that His Majesty will send each and every one of us his utmost thanks," said the ambassador for the Nebula Kingdom.

"I also accept. What say the both of you?" asked President Hackett.

"We accept," replied the ambassador for the Rock Syndicate.

"We accept," replied the ambassador for Qutalin.

"Excellent. I am happy to see that our negotiations have gone so well. While I have to unfortunately leave you in order to deal with some pressing business, the dessert that is coming up is exceptional. Feel free to enjoy as much as you want as you iron out the details amongst yourselves. Once you do so, send the treaty to my Secretary of State, and he will ensure that the legislature receives it promptly. If all goes well, you'll return home in a few days with a great document to show to your respective governments!"

The President got up from his chair after finishing his concluding remarks and left the presidential banquet hall. Walking the hallways toward his Presidential Office, he could not help but smile at all that he had accomplished so far. A decade of meticulous planning, a decade of excessive vetting of co-conspirators, a decade of painstaking attention to detail, a decade of allowing his men to be neglected by an administration that sought peace and domestic welfare at all costs. All in all, a decade of work and toil, and now President Hackett could enjoy the reward.

His purges of all the politicians and military officers who disagreed with his coup d'état have given President Hackett a fanatically loyal military. The officers revere and respect him, and the soldiers and sailors idolize him, hailing him as the hero who saved them all from over a decade of tyrannical mothballing. The Congress and Senate are now more or less relics of a bygone era, existing only to maintain the appearances of a republic and to add legitimacy to the decisions that the President unilaterally makes.

Furthermore, the dual combination of military victory and a robust augmentation of the domestic welfare system has given President Hackett a sky-high approval rating. It is rapidly approaching 80%, and there are no signs of it slowing down. The great failure of the domestic welfare policies under the Varis administration was not the result of the policies themselves; Admiral Hackett realized their genius from the moment that President Varis conceived of them, but rather the lack of funds. Not only did Admiral Hackett and other co-conspirators among the government secretly funnel funds away from the domestic welfare programs and into secret armament programs, but they also funneled money away and kept it in storage.

It was only a slight amount compared to the total amount of money that was currently in circulation, but even so, the money that had been siphoned away for over a decade has magically raced back into the economy in the form of domestic welfare. The economy was burning hotter than the sun, a great range of conquered space has been opened to unlimited development, and the Republic of Earth enjoyed a very powerful military, which grows bigger and bigger by the day.

All that was needed now, in order to begin realizing President Hackett's ambition of unifying all of humanity back into a single nation once again, was the acquisition of the Terraforming Installation. President Hackett was hopeful that the envelope he had just recently received would be one step closer to realizing that objective.

President Hackett arrived at his office and saluted the two presidential guards as they opened the doors for him. Walking inside the office, he still felt an overwhelming thrill of excitement over the fact that the Presidential Office was now *his* office; this thrill of joy came to him each and every time he entered the office, even though he had been President for quite some time. As the two presidential guards closed the doors behind him, he walked over to his chair and desk and took a seat. Opening the envelope on the Presidential Desk, he pulled out the folded sheet of paper and began to read.

It was a longer message than was normally the case for William; in fact, it was a longer message than was normally the case for any quantum message. Still, it was a message that brought great joy to President Hackett's eyes because the old captain shared the same eye for opportunity as he did. He was very happy about the fact that he had chosen William Nagy and his aging cruiser for this incredibly important mission.

President Hackett picked up the phone on his desk and called his main secretary. She picked up the phone almost immediately.

"Yes, Mr. President?" she asked.

"Get me in touch with the Admiralty Finance Division," replied President Hackett.

"Right away, sir, just one second."

The President could hear the secretary working the console in front of her until she got through to the Admiralty Finance Division. "Putting you through to them now, sir," said the main secretary.

The call was picked up immediately once the Admiral in charge of the Admiralty Finance Division saw the identity of the caller.

"Mr. President, it is an honor and privilege to be speaking with you," said the Admiral with deep respect.

"Thank you, Admiral; there is a small favor that I need you to do."

"Name it, sir."

"I need you to wire a sizeable number of quantum-backed crypto-credits to a cruiser that is currently on a deep frontier mission, alongside a message to be sent directly to the captain. Ship name: Shiny Moon. Wire amount: 5 million credits."

"I know the Shiny Moon well, sir; she's the little girl that could, filled with thousands of girls that definitely can!" said the Admiral, who could not help himself. The President laughed right alongside the Admiral for a brief moment before snapping back into focus.

"To the task at hand, Admiral."

"Yes, sir! I apologize."

"Don't apologize, Admiral; it was a damn good comment. Anyway, back to the task at hand: is it possible to wire such a large sum through quantum entanglement? I understand that we have some physics that get in the way."

"The signal technicians are going to throw a fit over the amount of work needed, but aye, it certainly can be done, sir. The physics dilemmas are not insurmountable. You also mentioned that you wanted a message sent directly to the captain; that can be done easily through computer permissions. What is the message that you want sent?"

The captain was busy daydreaming in his chair when the bosun interrupted his dreams. "Captain, the quantum signal technicians want you to head down to the quantum communications room."

"Tell them I'll be right down," ordered the captain, and he got up and left the bridge as the bosun carried out his orders.

Making his way from the bridge to the quantum communications room, the captain entered. Again, the signal technicians all got up and saluted while standing at attention.

"At ease, and you can refrain from doing so in the future; I don't particularly care about salutes or standing at attention," said the captain.

"Noted, sir. Regarding your previous order, we have a response from Admiral Hackett, although such a rank no longer applies to him," said one of the signal technicians.

"Oh? Then what rank applies?"

"Not a rank, a title. It is President Hackett now."

"I can't believe it!" said an astonished captain.

"The worst part is the only way that we are going to get more information about whatever has occurred back home is through quantum signals, and you know that protocol forbids casual communications that do not relate to the mission at hand," replied the signal technician.

"Unfortunately, it is as you say, sailor. While we are breaking half of the protocol rulebook on this mission, the book still applies with full force to the sailors back home. Anyway, what is the response from President Hackett?"

"Here it is, sir; it's addressed to Captain's Eyes only."

The captain got the sealed envelope from the signal technician and backtracked several steps until his back was against the far wall of the quantum communications room. Once there, he opened the sealed envelope, unfolded the paper inside, and began to read.

"Captain William Nagy, my favorite rascal in the fleet! I do not know if it is the bourbon that is no doubt flowing in your veins, assuming any of it has survived this far into your mission, or just that iron blood that only a veteran sailor has, but you and I share a similar eye. Your request is hereby approved, and I have authorized an additional sum in excess of the two million that you requested. You will have five million quantum-backed crypto-credits to spend as you wish on retrofitting your ship. I'm sure the amount will come in handy, especially if the nomads decide to play hardball during price negotiations—

Furthermore, I realize that you and your crew are no doubt starving for any news regarding the war that is going on, assuming, of course, that you have not heard about it; if I already mentioned it previously, then I apologize for forgetting. It was against the Solar Empire, and we have wrested from their hands a mighty victory. The Solarian menace is no more; we have destroyed their fleets, and we are presently occupying their worlds as we speak! This has opened up a great opportunity for us in so many ways, but regarding your mission, I've been able to allocate a few extra ships to head towards the far end of the Perseus arm; they should arrive in your sector of the galaxy very shortly—

Once they arrive, they will be able to assist you with your task, a task that I must stress is one of the most important missions that any ship in our great republic is ever going to undertake. If you succeed, as I am certain that you will, your name, alongside the name of your ship and crew, will live on for all time."

Captain Nagy folded the piece of paper back into the envelope and closed the envelope flap as he put the message in his pocket. His mind was racing with the dilemma of whether he should tell the crew of the victory or withhold the information. Whether he told the crew or not, the choice would have strong benefits but also some significant consequences. He finally made up his mind after a minute or two of agonizing thought.

"We won the war, gentlemen. The Solar Empire is no more."

The captain walked out of the room just as the enormity of his statement began to sink into the minds of the signal technicians. He smiled, overjoyed as the magnitude of the information he had just absorbed and shared with the signal technicians also made its way deep into his mind. He made up his mind then and there; he was not only going to tell his crew, but he was going to do so over the ship-wide loudspeaker. Landing on this planet was turning out to be the oasis stop of this half-year voyage.

The captain made his way to the bridge and wasted no time in taking a seat in his chair. His joyous demeanor raised the eyebrows of his first officer.

"Everything in order, sir?" asked the first officer.

"Indeed, first officer, indeed," replied the captain, who turned his head to look at the bosun.

"Bosun, open a ship-wide line from the bridge to every single loudspeaker that is fitted aboard our vessel."

The bosun, after a slight delay, replied, "Done, sir."

"Attention all hands of the Shiny Moon, this is your captain speaking. I have just received word from the Admiralty regarding a phenomenal event that has just occurred back home. We've conquered the Solar Empire!"

The captain paused his speech to let the information seep into the minds of every sailor and civilian aboard the vessel. After a short moment of silence, he continued.

"I, of course, do not need to say just how important this event is, not just for the security of our republic, but for the sector and galaxy at large! We are never going to have to fear invasion ever again. Great portions of our national budget can be used to finally improve our people, and not in the disgraceful form of the Varis administration's social programs. Furthermore, speaking of the Varis administration, we have a new president. By means that I am still trying to put together, Admiral Hackett—yes, our one and only Admiral Hackett of the 89th Reserve Fleet—has obtained the presidency."

"I know the man personally, and I can say for a fact that we are not in incompetent hands. All of us who were nervous for months regarding news about the war can now rest easy. We will have a home to go back to, that I can promise you. Finally, I can also promise you this: if we succeed in our mission and recover the Terraforming Installation that is our primary objective—as I am sure you have all heard by now—then we will be treated to a hero's welcome. Our republic won the war back home; now it is our job to bring home the spoils of a glorious tomorrow! Carry on!" finished the captain.

"Damn good speech, sir. All hail the sailors and soldiers who prevailed against the Solarian menace!" yelled out one of the ensigns who was seated in the gunnery suite of the bridge, and everyone yelled and cheered in celebration. The captain sat back and smiled at the sight.

Once the cheers began to die down, the captain turned to his first officer and said, "I'll be in my quarters; make sure the rascals don't burn down the ship in celebration before I get back."

"I'll do my best, sir!" replied the first officer with a smile as the captain got up from his chair and made his way to his quarters.

Once he arrived, Captain Nagy paused for a moment as he looked at the closed safe. He knew that inside was a bottle of fine bourbon, with glasses to share. He thought briefly about cracking the bottle open and taking a sip before passing it around the bridge, but he dismissed the thought as he sat down at his desk. Pulling out the communicator that the nomad mayor had given him, he made another call. It was picked up almost instantly.

"A pleasure as always, Captain," said the mayor.

"I have a business proposal for your planet."

"I'm listening."

"Is it possible to gather all of the different communities together, alongside your skills, and hire you for a more or less complete retrofit of my ship? We'll be paying in quantum-backed crypto-credits, but we'd pay well."

"It is certainly possible, but we've never done such an extensive retrofit before. Usually, a ship arrives at our world and obtains a specific replacement or repair. Otherwise, they come to trade. May I ask just how extensive the more or less complete retrofit that you are asking for is?"

"It's in the name; my ship needs to be cleaned and updated from the ground up. I am not asking for a miracle or even an upgrade, but the entire reason why we have no issues giving you our laser turrets in exchange for knowledge on the location of the Jalalight is that we cannot even use them if we wanted to. Our power wiring is not reliable enough to hold the current needed to safely operate them," said the captain with full honesty.

"I believe you, Captain, although I think you are getting the better end of our arrangement regarding the turrets. I do not know why the so-called civilized human nations continue to use laser weaponry. The range and speed are, of course, unmatched, but the actual firepower is abysmal."

"They have their uses; but I agree with you, railguns and missiles are the bread and butter of space warfare. Unless you have the energy of a sun, lasers can never hope to compete with those two weapon platforms."

Chapter Sixteen

"Exactly, those turrets will serve us better as mining drills," said the mayor. "Well, you have no disagreement on that point, mayor. Anyway, can my retrofit ambition be done? Or is it as improbable as the chance of me killing a Battleship-class vessel with just my laser turrets, assuming they were online, of course?" asked the captain.

"It can be done; I'll make a call and talk with the planetary governor as soon as we finish this call. But we are going to have to charge you a sizable sum. I do not think you have the quantum-backed crypto-credits aboard, even if you were to convince your entire crew to give them up in exchange for promissory notes."

"You can be surprised with such things. Let me know how the call with the planetary governor goes, mayor. Until then."

"Until then, captain." And the mayor concluded the call.

The captain returned to his duties on the bridge for the rest of the day and then retired for the night. He woke up early in the morning, eager to hear from the mayor regarding the possible retrofit and to see the results of the first day of shore leave. He got up, readied himself for the day, and went to the bridge. He walked to his chair; everything looked as normal as always.

"Anything new?" asked the captain.

"The first detachment of the crew on shore leave just left an hour ago," replied the first officer.

"So soon?"

"Yes, captain, the crew was 'insistent' on trying to move the slot forward so that another detachment or two can fit into today's schedule."

"Looks like we have a lack of patience and discipline aboard ship."

"That we do, sir. Then again, they haven't felt hard ground in over half a year; it is to be expected, especially among the civilians."

The captain remembered the currency dilemma and asked, "What about the computer technicians that are arriving with the quantum readers?"

"What, sir?" replied the first officer.

"Dammit, I forgot to brief the officers; what a sloppy mess."

"Well, you can start with me, captain. What is this quantum reader business that you referred to just now?"

The captain explained and debriefed the first officer, and he smiled as the captain provided the information. It was not as big of a deal as he was making it out to be.

"Ah, that. They arrived with the currency scanners a few hours ago, according to the night shift," said the first officer.

"The mayor contacted the ship?"

"Yes, they asked the head engineer to relay any communications to the bridge since they assumed that you were otherwise unavailable."

"They assumed correctly. What did they say?"

"That the quantum readers had arrived. It is what got the night shift to accelerate the shore leave deployments. I decided to continue with the decision once I took over for the day shift; I saw no reason to end it."

"Dammit, First Officer, why didn't you start with that when I asked if there was anything new?"

"Good point, sir. I blame the early morning."

The captain and the first officer continued to talk for a few more minutes; it was a pleasant conversation filled with laughter and humor. The mayor did not leave any word regarding retrofits, nor did he ask that the captain of the Shiny Moon contact him as soon as he was available. Because of this, the captain decided to wait until the afternoon before calling the mayor through the communicator in order to inquire about the status of the potential retrofit.

Near noon, before he could make the call himself, he received a call on the communicator, which he promptly took as he walked off the bridge and into the privacy of his quarters.

"Perfect, I was going to call you in an hour or two," said the captain as he answered the call.

"I have good news, Captain. The planetary governor just replied with news about your request for an extensive retrofit. He spoke with the other mayors, and they all agreed, so long as the necessary funds were available, to sell their services to you and your crew. Speaking of funds, you have three options: light touch-up, moderate retrofit, and extensive retrofit. We can do a light touch-up for 500,000 of your quantum-backed crypto credits; the moderate we can do for 2,500,000. As for the extensive retrofit, we have a rough estimate based on scans that we obtained as you approached our world. Your ship does seem to need an extensive retrofit; you have even admitted the fact to me regarding your electrical wiring. For the extensive retrofit, which is what you want and need, the fee is going to be 4,500,000 quantum-backed crypto-credits. Like we said, it is an amount that you likely do not have."

The captain was thrilled, not only at the fact that he could afford the extensive retrofit, but also that President Hackett decided to wire him 5 million, 3 million more than what he asked for initially. He had to at least attempt to keep up the appearances of military poverty, however.

"Can we drop the extensive retrofit to maybe 4 million?"

"No, captain, unfortunately, the price is fixed and non-negotiable."

"Alright, tell the rest of your settlements to begin the retrofit."

"Which one?"

"The extensive retrofit."

"Are you sure that you'll have the money for that?"

"We will; I give you my word on that."

"Alright, captain, I'll start to make the necessary calls."

The rest of the day went well. The crew that went on shore leave came back with great quantities of miscellaneous amenities. Rock and geode collections, as well as miscellaneous goods that the settlement had in stock in their local stores, were all purchased and brought back by an exuberant crew. The shore leave deployments came and went until nightfall, with everyone eager to return to the humble settlement that was the sole source of distraction within a reasonable distance of the ship.

The next day started exactly like the previous day. The shore leave deployment left the ship some two hours before Captain Nagy woke up, and the captain walked out of his quarters ready for another day of sitting in the captain's chair and twiddling his thumbs. Luckily, he was to be spared such misery. The communicator rang, and the captain answered the call without even bothering to get up from his chair; he was, after all, too lazy that morning to walk back to his quarters for privacy.

"Captain, are you busy at this time?" asked the mayor.

"No, I assume the same for you?" replied the captain.

"You assume correctly, captain."

"What is it that you need?"

"I want to invite you personally for a round at our local bar, assuming, of course, that such a thing would not be a problem for you."

The first officer stared at the captain with a grin; the captain caught his stare and responded to it with a frown.

"No, it will not be a problem, but I'm not much of a drinker," replied the captain, and the first officer nearly burst out laughing before he managed to restrain himself.

"I see. Well, we have some drinks with glucose mixed in; that should be right up your alley," said the mayor, with a tone that almost sounded like mockery.

"That would be lovely. When do you want to have this little meeting?"

"Right now, captain. I am in one of our transports directly outside your ship. Join me when you are ready," replied the mayor, and he hung up.

"I'm not much of a drinker, my ass, sir!" yelled the first officer, which caused the entire bridge to roar with laughter.

"Ah, shut it. You have the bridge. Oh, one more thing, first officer, I need an officers' meeting when I get back. It is alright if we miss some of them if they are presently on their shore leave deployment, but try to get as many as you can to show up."

"Meeting topic is the extensive retrofit that we just purchased from the nomads, I presume?" asked the first officer, who had heard the entire conversation between the captain and the mayor on the communicator.

"You presume correctly. Get to it."

"Yes, sir."

The captain left the bridge. First, he took the elevator down to the sensor deck of the ship. Once there, he went over to the quantum communications room and instructed the signal technicians, who were currently in possession of the enormous number of quantum-backed crypto-credits, to authorize their distribution. The only two officers allowed to wire the funds will be the first officer and himself. This is solely to compensate the nomads for the services rendered related to the ship retrofit that was soon to commence. The transactions are to be recorded, along with the name of the individual who authorized them, and compiled into a list that will later be sent back to the Admiralty, alongside any remaining unspent credits. Once he did so, he left the quantum communications room and took the elevator down to the ground deck.

After donning one of the oxygen tanks with the attached plastic mask, the captain entered the airlock chamber and left the ship through the other side. Walking down the staircase until he stepped onto the soil of the nomad world, he looked around until he found the mayor's transport, then proceeded to walk toward it until he reached it. The door opened, and the captain entered the transport. He took a seat next to the mayor; as soon as he did so, the pilot lifted off from the ground and started to make his way to the settlement. Everyone aboard the transport wore supplemental oxygen masks.

"So, do you wear supplemental oxygen indoors?" asked the captain.

"Oh, gods no, captain! Each building that you enter has an airlock-like room, where you then open another door before entering. After all, the atmosphere is breathable; it's just not survivable for more than an hour or two," replied the mayor.

"I see. Isn't your problem simply a lack of oxygen and pressure?"

"You nailed it, captain. Originally, this world was dead, in a decent enough spot in the habitable zone around this star but lacking in atmosphere and magnetic field. More or less, it was a larger version of Mars, back before your nation terraformed it into the rough copy of Earth that it is today."

"I don't think that's correct, mayor."

"Oh? You're a historian as well as a captain now?"

"Definitely not a historian; I could never deal with all the reading necessary for that job. But Mars was terraformed under The Human Unity before it split off into the thousands of different nations that now encompass human civilization across the galaxy. In a way, it was 'our' nation that terraformed it into the rough copy of Earth that it is today," said the captain.

"Fine, 'our' nation then, Captain."

"Anyways, why don't you send a diplomatic mission over to the Republic of Earth? We do have some decent terraforming technology; maybe you can get a good deal on some equipment, especially with all the money that has just been injected into your economy!" suggested the Captain.

"That won't happen," replied the Mayor plainly.

"Why not?"

"Captain, I know it is difficult for you to understand, but our way of life is completely against the one that predominates in your nation. You pay lip service to the ideals of liberty, freedom, and general autonomy with regard to the state. You call yourselves a republic, but your state rules over you all the same. You say that you are a democracy, but when was the last time that you directly voted for something that was actually implemented?"

"I said to buy terraforming technology, not to join the republic!"

"I know what you said, Captain, but by entering talks with the Republic, we acknowledge its legitimacy. Not only do we put ourselves on the map, more than what we already did by accepting your arrival on our world, but we also invite prospectors and other opportunists who would want nothing more than to buy our world for cheap, then sell it back to us for a fortune later. It will take centuries more before we can breathe our world's air without the need to supplement it with a mask, but it will be our world, free of any outside influence. And it is what we value most."

"I see, Mayor, and I understand."

"I mean no disrespect, of course, Captain, and we are willing to bend our own stance somewhat; after all, we certainly don't mind the outside influence of 4.5 million of your credits! Not to mention all of the credits that your crew is dropping in my settlement," said the Mayor with a smile.

"I'm sure that it'll do you very nicely!" replied the Captain.

The transport continued in its flight path until it arrived at the settlement. The pilot slowly descended and landed the transport on a large flat rectangular parking lot alongside other transports, which were currently idle.

"I'm assuming the current portion of my crew that is on shore leave deployment is scattered all across this humble settlement?" asked the captain, who was taking in the view through the window as the transport finished its landing.

"They certainly are! No doubt they are buying things that we just can't stop laughing about," replied the mayor as the transport doors opened, and both of them stepped outside and started to walk toward the settlement.

"What sort of things?"

"Rocks, geodes, other things that for us are all but useless. They are pretty to look at and display; however, quite a lot of your crew is buying them."

"I have no doubt about that, Mayor."

"It must've been a long while since your ship has gotten shore leave."

"Almost half a year," replied the captain.

"That explains everything then," added the mayor.

The staffer raced into the emergency war meeting that was called by the president, carrying documents that he quickly placed in front of an admiral before darting out of the room just as quickly as he entered. President Hackett continued to speak as he did so.

"The trade agreement is going to make our people rich, but it will anger the other three nations that are participating in it. We've gotten major concessions from them through the lucky roll of the fortune dice, but this is not going to last forever; hence my new ambitions," said President Hackett.

"But Mr. President, to sufficiently build up our military in order to carry out said ambition, I don't see how it is possible given the timeline that you proposed and the sheer number of resources and energy stockpiles that would be needed," replied one of the generals, who was not convinced.

"General, your men especially have done an excellent job at conquering the last stubborn holdouts of the Solar Empire. I wish to thank you and your men for such an important task."

"Thank you for those words, Mr. President, but returning to the matter at hand, I still can't see your plan becoming a reality."

"What about all of the space that we conquered? The great fleets of Solarian ships that now lie destroyed, unable to disembark in time before their destruction? The resources will be there, especially once we have an unlimited number of worlds upon which we can live," added President Hackett.

"If we have an unlimited number of worlds, Mr. President, we still don't know if the Shiny Moon will be able to locate the Terraforming Installation," said one of the admirals.

"They are getting closer. The most recent message we received from them indicated that they are currently on a nomad world, and they have bargained for information regarding the Jalalight in exchange for their offline laser turrets."

"But, Mr. President, you of all people know that we have to think about the worst possible scenario when we think about strategy, especially when your newly proposed strategy is to beef up our military until we can take over the entire galaxy," said the general, who still was not on board.

"Alright, how many ships and soldiers do we need then?"

"It's not a matter of ships, Mr. President, but instead the people needed to crew them and the public support necessary to justify war after war. We got lucky in our most recent war and bluffed The Solar Empire completely and utterly, winning with little effort. The people are ecstatic because of it, hence your sky-high approval rating and the high level of support for this government. The moment that we head into war after war without end, however, all of that will change for the worse. Why do you even want to attempt to do this?"

"Because we are never going to progress as a species if we don't!" President Hackett raised his voice, not because of anger, but because of the intense passion he had for this subject. "All throughout history, the best moments were when humanity was united. The Chinese dynasties, the Roman Empire, and all the other empires of Earth forced the development of humanity forward. Case in point is the Terraforming Installation itself! We have no idea how to make it; the only reason it exists is because of The Human Unity!"

"But the cost of unifying all of humanity under military force!"

"Are unacceptable, I know. I want the strongest military in the galaxy only as a last resort, in case my other, more clandestine strategies do not work. After all, you yourself said that I, of all people, should know that you have to think about the worst possible scenario when you think about strategy."

"I stand corrected, Mr. President; I apologize for doubting your ambitions," said the general, who saw that the president only intended for war as a last resort.

"Your apology is accepted, General," replied the president with a smile.

Chapter Seventeen

"Alright, tell me that again, you mine with pickaxes?" asked Captain Nagy in utter disbelief.

"Not entirely; we'd be mining the ore vein for centuries if that were the case! But the hard-to-reach areas, which we cannot melt with our small lasers, those we need to clear by hand. Usually, it is with a handheld drill, but sometimes you need the fine point that only a pickaxe can give you," replied the mayor as he took another sip of his watered-down beer.

"I see," said the captain, drinking water with glucose.

"How's the fruit juice?"

"It's good, although I would disagree with the statement that this is fruit juice. It is water, glucose, and some chemicals that give it the taste of some horrible version of fruit punch. Doesn't even have red dye in it."

"I should get you a beer then, unless you're a total teetotaler."

"You mean that watered-down mix? It's probably worse than whatever I'm currently drinking."

"So, when did you stop drinking?"

"Six months ago, right before I got deployed on my current mission. Having the captain dazed with alcohol while on the job is not a good sign for the longevity of the ship and her crew."

"To sober captains!" toasted the mayor, and the two men clinked their glasses before taking another sip.

"I'm assuming that this beer is made on-world?"

"From greenhouse hops!" replied the mayor with pride.

"Bartender!" yelled out Captain Nagy, and the bartender came over.

"Yes?" he replied.

"Get me one beer; I need to see what greenhouse hops taste like," said the captain.

"They taste the same as any other frontier beer," replied the bartender.

"I'm more of an inner-planet kind of person," replied the captain, and the bartender poured the nomad planet beer into a glass before handing it to the captain.

"What form of currency are you paying with?"

"I need to pay?" asked the captain, pushing the glass away from him.

"No, you don't; no one pays for this piss," said the bartender with a smile, sliding the glass back to the captain.

"So, it's free for everyone?"

"How do you think we get through the day?" added the mayor.

The captain took a sip of the beer, and to say that it was horrible would be an understatement. He put the glass down and slid it over to the mayor.

"Between the fruit juice, which I swear is just wastewater from the local mine, and whatever horrendous combination of hops, water, and chemicals is in the beer that I just drank, I don't know which one is worse," said the captain with full honesty.

"Give it here," said the mayor, who took the glass and drank it all in just a few moments.

"Tell me, mayor, what is this planet going to look like in a century?"

"Planning to start a life here?"

"No, but your world is going to eventually grow in size. I do not see your government system surviving when you have billions upon billions of people on this world."

"It will look the same as it does now. The only difference is that there will be more people, and the air will be better. If we are fortunate, we will have many plants all over the place, maybe even forests."

"A fair enough answer."

The captain and the mayor continued to talk for a few more hours until the conversation covered everything it could possibly cover. Once it reached such a point, the captain was flown back to his ship, and he thanked the mayor for the pleasant start to his day before heading through the ship's airlock and back to his chair. The rest of the day was more or less uneventful.

The retrofit itself took around three weeks. Every day was a great whine of noise for the Shiny Moon and the crew that had the misfortune of being onboard. Electrical wiring was stripped and replaced, supplementary power cores were cleaned and overhauled, and anything that could be replaced by a newer or better version of the same part that was in stock on the nomad world was replaced without any hesitation. The Shiny Moon got several new railguns, crude designs that were popular out in the frontier, but they were better than not having them at all in the first place.

Furthermore, the empty turret slots were converted into missile silos. The missile warhead capacity aboard the ship was expanded, and several missiles that the nomads had in surplus were given to the Shiny Moon to bolster her arsenal. She had permanently lost her laser turrets, but in exchange gained a sizable increase in firepower, enough to possibly classify her as a battlecruiser.

"Here's your communicator, Mayor; it has been a lovely three weeks. I won't miss the retrofit noise, but I'll definitely miss your world," said Captain Nagy, handing the mayor the communicator that he had been given.

"It was a great three weeks as well. We received the last of the funds yesterday from your first officer; those funds, combined with the spending that your crew did on shore leave, are enough for us to invest seriously in infrastructure all across our world. We may even get an official spaceport instead of a few landing pads and the mountains as an exhaust shield," replied the mayor.

"A spaceport sounds like a good idea; then again, I'm sure you'll come up with the best investment for your world at the present time."

"Come back at any time if you are in the sector, Captain."

"Will do, Mayor. Until then." The two men shook hands and tapped each other on the back before the captain left and went through the airlock for the last time.

Heading straight for the bridge, the captain wasted no time.

"Alright, everyone, what's our status for launch?" asked the captain.

"Green, sir; just waiting for the nomads to pass the mountain peak and reach a safe distance," replied the helmsman.

"Sounds good. Bosun, sound liftoff stations."

"Yes, sir! Attention all hands, please man your liftoff stations. Attention all hands, please man your liftoff stations," said the bosun, his orders echoing by loudspeaker all across the ship.

The captain waited until the head sensor officer informed the bridge that the nomads had just passed the exhaust danger zone before beginning takeoff procedures.

"They are clear, sir; we can proceed," said the head sensor officer.

"Bosun, open a line to all ship departments," ordered the captain.

"Already done, sir," replied the bosun.

"Engineering, status?"

"Green, Captain," replied the head engineer.

"Sensor suite, status?"

"Green, Captain," replied the head sensor officer.

"Gunnery suite, status?"

"Green, Captain," replied the head gunnery officer.

"All departments ready, Captain," added the bosun.

"Keep all lines open, Helmsman. Get us off this rock and set course for the Jalalight, maximum warp," ordered the Captain.

"Gladly, sir! T-minus 10 on your order," replied the Helmsman.

"Go."

"T-minus 10, 9, 8, 7, 6, 5, 4, 3, 2, 1. Launch!"

Unlike the chemical rocket-assisted launch back on Earth, this launch started with a bang. Even at minimal torch thrust, the ship kicked and roared upwards, easily countering the minimal air resistance and gravity that had no hope of slowing down her ascent.

"Continue with minimal torch until we reach the upper atmosphere. I don't want to scar the mountain range with plasma any more than what we have to in order to get into space," ordered the Captain.

"Yes, sir. I will only accelerate before then if we begin to decline in altitude," replied the Helmsman.

The ship had no need of accelerating before then; she effortlessly climbed in altitude until she reached the outer bands of the atmosphere. Activating the gravity deck plates and the inertial stabilizers and dampeners, the ship prepared itself for space cruising.

"Alright, Helm. Once the compartments rotate into place, activate regular departure drive," ordered the Captain.

"Yes, sir," replied the Helmsman.

The compartments began to rotate into place, and for a minute, one could feel a slight falling sensation combined with a sense of rocking—the same rocking sensation that one can feel on a small boat that floats on the ocean. After the minute passed, the decks locked into place, and once again the crew could feel the sensation of gravity, as if they were standing on Earth.

"Alright, Helm. 10% torch engine capacity, followed by 25% when we are sufficiently away from the nomad world. Set course for the nearest Lagrange point, and get us into FTL as soon as possible," ordered the Captain.

"Yes, sir," replied the Helmsman.

"Engineering, get the FTL warper engines online and ready for activation as soon as the Helm reaches the Lagrange point."

"Yes, sir," replied the head engineer.

One could not feel the change in acceleration, but the ship jumped and rapidly gained in velocity as it approached the Lagrange point. As the Shiny Moon continued to approach the Lagrange point of the nomad world, she received an incoming transmission.

"Sir, the nomad world is contacting us," said the head sensor officer.

"Put them through," replied the captain.

"Yes, sir."

"Shiny Moon, I appreciate that you rocketed off conservatively from our world; not everyone is as considerate as you in such matters," said the planetary governor.

"Ah, planetary governor, I remember our last conversation well," replied the captain.

"As do I. Your suggestion regarding the construction of a terraforming industry on our world has been noted and will definitely be debated in the near future."

"I'm glad to hear it. I understand that you are reluctant to trade with other nations that do not share your governing ethos. Because of that, I strongly recommend that you develop your own industry. Hopefully, that small injection of money into your economy can get the ball rolling."

"Only time will tell us the answer to that, captain. Anyway, I just wanted to wish you and your crew a bon voyage. I hope that the Jalalight has the answers and knowledge that you seek."

"As do I, governor. Be well." After the captain wished the governor well, the nomad planet terminated the line.

The Shiny Moon continued to head towards the Lagrange point before finally reaching it. Slowing down until she was at a standstill, she prepared her FTL warpers for activation and roared into FTL as soon as possible. The most probable location for the Jalalight was only a week away at maximum FTL.

"FTL path stable, captain. We are exiting the solar system now."

"Thank you, helmsman. Bosun, stand everyone down; regular stations."

"Yes, captain."

The rest of the day was uneventful. The crew began to return to the old routines that they had perfected over six months, and the captain sat back and relaxed in his chair, using the slight hum of the bulkheads at FTL as a source of calm for his meditation. Everyone else continued to man their consoles, keeping the ship on course and ensuring that all of her systems were running at optimal efficiency.

As initially predicted, it took just over a week for the Shiny Moon to arrive at the supposed location of the Jalalight. It was a very faint nebula; the gases had, for the most part, dissipated after countless millennia, but enough gas remained to hide a ship from sensors. A perfect hiding spot, without much of the more harmful effects that a thicker nebula would have upon a ship.

"Anything that may be of interest, head sensor officer?" asked the captain.

"There is a solar system near the leftmost edge," replied the head sensor officer through a communication line.

"Helmsman, set course," ordered the captain.

"Right away, captain."

The ship inched toward the system at minimal FTL, the only safe speed whenever one wishes to warp space filled with gas around a ship. Arriving at the outermost edge of the system, the Shiny Moon stopped.

"Is this solar system populated?" asked the captain.

"Yes, sir, a few small planetoids; an irregular object is orbiting one of them near the center of the system," replied the head sensor officer.

"Alright then; head gunnery officer, standard defensive posture; helmsman, send a standard Republic of Earth greeting, and take us in slowly."

"Yes, captain," replied the head gunnery officer.

"Yes, captain," replied the helmsman.

The Shiny Moon raised her shields and began to approach the planetoid with the irregular object that was currently orbiting it at normal torch speed. The standard Republic of Earth greeting was received by the irregular object, and it responded with a reply.

"State your intentions," said the Jalalight.

"Pursuit of knowledge," replied the Shiny Moon.

The Shiny Moon slowed down before coming to a complete stop in order to allow the Jalalight to position herself defensively, without the pressure of having to react to an unknown ship approaching her from the outer system.

"We offer knowledge, but you must provide knowledge in return."

"What kind of knowledge are you looking for, Jalalight?"

"It depends on the value of the knowledge that you seek from us."

"We are looking for a particular 'ship'; it can turn a world from barren rock into paradise. It goes by the name: Terraforming Installation."

"That is a high value to demand; we need something equal."

The captain paused for a moment and began to contemplate just what could be valuable enough to give to the ship in exchange for such information. He turned to his first officer.

"Any ideas, First Officer?" asked the captain.

"Not a single one," replied the first officer.

"Bosun, tell the Jalalight that we are going to be delayed in responding; we need to analyze our stores of knowledge and find something that can equal the value of knowing the location of the Terraforming Installation," ordered the captain.

"Right away, sir," replied the bosun.

The bosun wrote up a message and sent it to the Jalalight; they responded quickly.

"We will wait gladly for your response," the Jalalight said.

"Alright, officer's meeting on the bridge. If anyone within earshot of our little conversation has something to add, no matter how stupid the idea, I want to hear it," ordered the captain.

"Do we have any technology that they could want?" asked the civilian liaison.

"Doubtful, and if we did have something valuable, naval protocols dictate that we do not share it," replied the head gunnery officer.

"Frankly, this rust bucket has nothing of value to share. Unless the inhabitants out here on the frontier have a pitiful technological base, anything that we have aboard in the technological sense has been outdated for decades. Furthermore, the nomads back on that planet no doubt took detailed scans of our ship; if we have anything valuable, it has long since been shared," added the head engineer.

"What about the biological samples?" suggested the head doctor.

"Dammit, Doctor, that's ingenious! DNA from life seeded by the Terraforming Installation; they are going to have to accept that!" said the captain.

"The only issue is the DNA is still raw. The data has not yet been organized into a legible or useful form," replied the head doctor.

"Still, it's a good trade; we need something else, however, to really seal the deal in my eyes," said the first officer.

Just then, the captain's eyes opened wide in excitement.

Chapter Eighteen

"Dammit, I have it," said the captain out loud.

"Please elaborate, sir," replied the head sensor officer.

"Bosun, tell the Jalalight that we have two separate pieces of knowledge to exchange for the knowledge of the Terraforming Installation's current location: DNA from organisms handcrafted by the Terraforming Installation itself and a bottle of fine bourbon brewed on Earth. The contents of the bottle could be analyzed and replicated out here in the frontier," ordered the captain, and the bosun sent the message without delay.

"The bourbon, how exclusive is it?" asked the Jalalight.

"It is consumed by the Admiralty of our navy. It is hard to find on Earth; as such, it is priceless out here in the frontier," said the captain.

After a slight delay, the Jalalight responded, "We accept your trade; bring the bottle and the DNA data with you on a shuttle. We will give you instructions on how to dock with us once your shuttle is in range."

"Understood, Jalalight; talk to you then," replied the captain, and the bosun sent the message on over.

"Head doctor, send with me a few of your non-essential personnel who understand and can sell the DNA that we have to the Jalalight. I'll join them shortly at the entrance to the shuttle bay," ordered the captain.

"It'll be more or less the same people from last time; I'll give you two genetic specialists," replied the head doctor.

"That's perfect; we don't need more than three people to deliver express cocktail service followed by data," said the captain with a chuckle.

"Indeed, captain," replied the head doctor, who was laughing as well.

The captain got up and walked over to his captain's quarters. Opening the safe that held the bourbon bottle, he very carefully untied the attached glasses and picked up the bottle with both hands. He hugged it tightly against his right shoulder, with his right hand supporting it on the bottom and his left hand helping to press it tightly against his chest. Once he secured the bottle, he locked the safe, left his quarters, and returned to the bridge.

Once there, he gave control of the ship to the first officer and raced down the decks toward the shuttle deck. Stepping off the elevator, he walked briskly yet carefully toward the entrance to the shuttle bay. The shuttle bay was pressurized, and the shuttle pilot had been called; he was getting into the cockpit just as the captain arrived.

Still slightly ahead of the genetic specialists, the captain walked up to the shuttle and got in. The pilot decided to engage in small talk.

"Cocktail service, sir?" he asked, seeing the bottle nestled in the captain's arm.

"Something like that, pilot," replied the captain.

"I see. Well, they better enjoy it, sir. After all, we certainly won't."

"I agree with you completely, pilot."

The captain and the pilot waited for a few more moments until the genetic specialists arrived. They each carried a computer alongside a small bag that no doubt contained different data transfer devices, one of which was bound to be compatible with the computers aboard the Jalalight.

"Ready to depart, captain?" asked the pilot.

"Ready. In addition, minimal g-force maneuvers, pilot; if I drop this bottle, the mission that we have just spent half a year or more pursuing will end in failure," replied the captain.

"As gentle as a feather; that is how much g-force you'll feel, captain."

The pilot did not lie. Once the bridge opened the shuttle bay doors, the pilot eased the shuttle out of the bay using only RCS thrusters. Turning the shuttle to face the direction of the Jalalight, it took a while for the shuttle to ramp up speed, the pilot being extra gentle on the controls. Slowly but surely, the shuttle made its way to the Jalalight.

Once she was close enough, the shuttle began to slow down. A message was sent from the Jalalight to the shuttle, informing them of the specific shuttle bay they were to enter. The pilot slowly made his way to the Jalalight and then orbited the ship until the shuttle bay was located. Easing the shuttle in slowly, the bay doors opened, and a few moments after that, the shuttle landed on the shuttle bay floor of the Jalalight, and the doors closed behind it.

The settlement on the nomad world that just a week ago had been busy with tourists from the Shiny Moon was up in smoke. The vast majority of its residents were dead or dying; their pitiful attempts at resistance had proven utterly useless against the invading foe. The mayor, who was gravely wounded by a ripper round that went through his left shoulder, crawled into his office and pulled down a bookshelf with his only remaining shoulder to plug the door and prevent it from opening.

Using the coagulating injections in the first aid kit in his office, the mayor successfully stopped the bleeding at the cost of his left arm tingling with numbness. If he did not receive extensive medical attention, his arm would have to be amputated. Loading his rifle with a fresh magazine of rounds, he waited until the invaders found his office; he wanted to take a few of them with him to the grave.

It took a few minutes, but the blood trail the mayor left behind was obvious. The sounds of war had died down. More or less, the entire settlement was either captured, dead, or dying. The mayor saw a quick flash, followed by a great cloud of splinters as the door and bookshelf were destroyed with great kinetic force. The mayor unloaded his rifle's magazine at the fully automatic setting, directing a cloud of bullets toward the door. Yet it did not do a single thing; the heavily armored marine, who was wearing a power suit, walked into the office without a scratch.

The mayor tried to pull the pistol from his right side to kill himself and thus prevent his capture and inevitable interrogation, but the marine effortlessly skipped toward him and grabbed his arm before he could do so. The incredibly strong grip broke the mayor's right arm, and he cried out in pain as he dropped the pistol. The mayor was more or less completely defenseless at this point, with a dead left arm from the ripper round wound and now a dead right arm due to his two broken radius and ulna bones.

"There you are. I'm disappointed in you, Mayor. You are the leader of this settlement, and all you can do when she is under attack is cower away in what is no doubt your office. Utterly shameful; you are just like the cowardly politicians that we liquidated back home," said the marine in disgust as he picked up the mayor by his torso and carried him outside.

The rest of the invading marines were waiting for their compatriot outside the building. They were pleased when they saw him emerge with the target in hand.

"Here he is, Lieutenant; I caught him hiding away like a coward in his office," replied the marine, placing the objective on the ground.

"Typical politician. Anyway, nice work, marine. Sergeant, bring him to the attack lander and make sure that he is stabilized enough that he'll survive liftoff," ordered the lieutenant.

"Yes, Lieutenant!" replied the sergeant, picking up the mayor as if he were a small dog and carrying him at high speed to the attack lander.

"I reckon we cleared the settlement," said the marine.

"Oh yes, we did, marine; it was much easier than the simulations aboard ship—a waste of time for the most part. They still used regular rifled bullets; subjugating the last of these vermin once President Hackett gives us an all clear is going to be a vacation," replied the lieutenant with a cruel laugh.

"Want us to head back to the attack lander?" asked another marine.

"We might as well; head back to the attack lander, everyone," ordered the lieutenant, and the marines complied, running back to the attack lander at great speed.

The lieutenant joined them, and within a few short moments, they had arrived. The mayor was restrained in place and stabilized by the sergeant, and immediately after the lieutenant gave the pilot the go-ahead, the attack lander roared off the surface and effortlessly climbed the atmosphere until reaching space. Once there, the miniature torch engines fired and rocketed the attack lander toward the small fleet of five advanced Republic of Earth cruisers that single-handedly conquered the nomad world.

The shuttle docked, and the mayor was carried off to an interrogation room. Once there, he was restrained onto a solid metal table, and then the table was rotated so that the mayor was upright. The lieutenant, who was now in regular sailing uniform, and the captain of the cruiser in which he was stationed, watched from the end of the room as the interrogators started to get to work. They wasted no time and opened their briefcases, revealing a great number of different tools designed for one purpose only: to force knowledge out of the mind of someone unwilling to give it up.

"We know that you are not a foolish man, so we are going to be plain with you. We can keep you alive under the most hellish conditions for years; all men eventually break, no matter how strong their willpower is, after all. Because of this, you have a choice: you can tell us the information now and be executed while you sleep soundly, or you can spend the rest of your conscious moments in agony and be executed whenever we feel like it once you ultimately tell us the knowledge that we want to know," said the torturer.

"Well, get to it then, you bastard backstabbing Earthian bastards!" retorted the mayor, who spat at the interrogator.

The blast of spit hit the interrogator straight in the face. He did not flinch or even move; instead, he walked over to his briefcase and picked up a towel. Dousing it with rubbing alcohol, he cleaned and sterilized his face with the towel before picking up the first of the torture devices that would be used to force the knowledge out of the mayor.

"Very well, let's not waste any time then." The interrogator pressed a button on the torture device he picked up, which turned it on and caused it to emit a menacing whirl. "What is the location of the Jalalight?"

The mayor withstood the torture for four days, a strong showing since the average human only lasts for three days at the utmost before succumbing to the agony and pain. After a few days of additional torture as punishment for daring to spit in the face of the interrogator at the beginning, the mayor was executed by ejection from an airlock while still fully conscious.

"Message sent, sir. The Admiralty and the other hunter fleets have been given the location of the Jalalight," relayed the ship's bosun.

"Perfect. Helmsman, set course for the Jalalight, maximum warp," ordered the captain.

"Right away, sir," replied the helmsman.

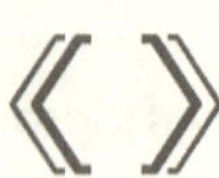

"Sir, we have the location of the Jalalight," said an admiral.

"Good. I trust that the nomad world was not that difficult to deal with?" asked President Hackett with a smile.

"It was not difficult at all, sir. They initially wanted extra payment, telling us that the deal with the Shiny Moon applied exclusively to the Shiny Moon. They still thought that they were dealing with the old Republic of Earth. They learned quickly of their error."

"Excellent. The report mentioned that we are going to redirect one of the fleets that is en route to the outer edge of the Perseus Arm to garrison the solar system. I was curious as to the reason."

"The world has a surprisingly rich atmosphere. It is not survivable without an oxygen mask that provides supplementary oxygen, but it is of high enough pressure that one can walk around with just a supplementary oxygen mask. It would make for a great forward operating base for our newest frontier fleet. In addition, it can be easily terraformed at a later date."

"That is a good reason and a good call as well, Admiral. Nice work."

"Thank you, Mr. President. I was certain that you would agree with it."

Captain Nagy and the two genetic specialists got out of the shuttle. An individual emerged from an open door and walked toward them.

"Welcome to the Jalalight!" said the individual, who bowed slightly in a show of respect.

"Thank you for having us! We come with knowledge to trade," said Captain Nagy, gesturing at the bourbon bottle and at the two genetic specialists, who each carried a computer and a small bag.

"I see. With me, please," ordered the individual, and Captain Nagy and the two genetic specialists followed the individual as the four of them left the shuttle bay.

The four individuals walked through the corridors of the Jalalight until they arrived at a room that was full of computer servers. A few marines were on sentry guard, followed by several technicians who were clearly waiting for the guests and the gifts of knowledge that they brought.

"Here we are!" said the individual with a smile.

"Bring the bourbon bottle here," ordered one of the technicians, and Captain Nagy complied.

The captain handed the bottle to the technician, who immediately placed it in a scanner. The scanner got to work, analyzing every single possible detail. Once the scanner finished with the scans, the technician opened the bottle of bourbon and poured some of the contents into a liquid analyzer. The analyzer took a few minutes to analyze, but once it finished, the technician smiled.

"The exact chemical composition has been obtained!" said the technician with a smile.

"So, you can replicate the bourbon exactly?" asked Captain Nagy.

"Indeed, a great gift of knowledge; we thank you for it," replied the technician.

"They still have another gift to give us, a specific DNA sequence," said the individual.

"Interesting, well I'm certainly not going to say no to more gifts of knowledge. In what format do you have the data stored?" asked the technician.

One of the genetic specialists from the Shiny Moon stepped forward: "Do you have a Wi-Fi router?"

"Ancient technology, but yes, we do," replied the technician, who quickly darted out of the room and into a closet.

The technician rummaged through the closet, and after a few moments, he emerged with a device in hand. Plugging it into a computer socket, he turned it on.

"Device ID is A-65," said the technician aloud.

The genetic specialist connected to the router and transferred the files over. The technician saw the files and quickly opened and scanned them. Seeing that they were raw DNA code in the ATGC format, he scanned the files with a DNA reader; the reader only took a few moments before it started to display relevant information.

"Fascinating, this is a great gift!" said the technician.

"You now have the ability to brew fine bourbon, and you know of some unique combinations that DNA can come in. We now ask for the location of the Terraforming Installation," said Captain Nagy with full sincerity.

"Of course, ironically enough, it was the Terraforming Installation that came to us with a favor," replied the technician.

"A favor?" asked the captain with a tone of surprise.

"Yes, a favor. I have to say that the team that designed it was incredibly bright; I would say too bright for our species. The vessel is perfection: beautiful, powerful, and incredibly wise," replied the technician, who had nothing but absolute admiration for the Terraforming Installation.

"What was the favor that the Terraforming Installation asked of you?"

"Ah, I apologize. The favor was quite simple: in exchange for some star charts that we particularly wanted, we were to sit in this faint nebula and await the arrival of a vessel called 'Shiny Moon.' Once this vessel arrived, we were to tell you the exact location of the Terraforming Installation."

"How does it know?" asked the captain, who was starting to get an uneasy feeling near the back of his neck.

"It's an AI; it knows things that we cannot even begin to comprehend. Just one second," replied the technician, who picked up a wired phone and dialed the Jalalight bridge.

After a brief conversation, the technician hung up the phone.

"Alright, the bridge is sending your ship the exact coordinates; your helmsman should not have any issues finding the solar system where your objective awaits," said the technician.

"We'll be going then; it was nice meeting you," replied the captain.

"One last thing," said the technician just as Captain Nagy and the two genetic specialists were heading out of the room.

"What is it?" replied Captain Nagy, who turned around.

"I don't know what your mission is. I do not even know why the Terraforming Installation wants you to find it. I just ask that you treat one of mankind's greatest achievements with respect. It would pain me greatly to hear that you disabled her just to rip her apart and analyze her contents."

"We will be doing nothing of the sort."

"I'm glad to hear it; thank you for the twin gifts of knowledge!"

"And thank you for the location of the Terraforming Installation."

Chapter Nineteen

With the information that the Shiny Moon had been waiting for now in hand, Captain Nagy and the two genetic specialists who accompanied him to the Jalalight raced back to the shuttle. They arrived, wished farewell to the individual aide who had been escorting them, and boarded the shuttle. The pilot was ordered to return to the Shiny Moon at full speed.

"Copy that, sir," replied the pilot as he roared the shuttle out of the shuttle bay and straight towards the Shiny Moon.

The captain pulled out a remote communicator from his pocket and dialed the bridge. The bosun picked up the call almost instantly.

"Yes, captain?"

"Did you receive the coordinates from the Jalalight yet?"

"Received and punched in, sir. We are ready to head to the nearest Lagrange point and enter FTL as soon as you come back."

"Sounds good, bosun. Have the helmsman make his way to the Lagrange point and call for FTL stations as soon as we enter the shuttle bay."

"Yes, sir."

It did not take long for the shuttle to arrive back home. Like clockwork, the moment that the shuttle landed on the shuttle bay bulkheads and was unified with the artificial gravity generated by the gravity deck plates, the helmsman activated full torch drive and headed to the nearest Lagrange point. The speed was great, and the ship was slowing down and preparing for FTL right as the captain arrived at the bridge.

"Everyone ready for FTL insertion?" asked the captain while taking a seat.

"All departments ready, captain," replied the bosun.

"Perfect. Helmsman, get us into FTL."

"Yes, sir!"

A few hours after the Shiny Moon departed the solar system, a fleet of Republic of Earth cruisers arrived. In just a few seconds, they detected the Jalalight and approached the target at maximum torch drive. Weapon systems and shields were online just a few seconds after that.

"Captain, the target has been located. We'll be in firing range in just a few minutes," said the helmsman of the ship as he continued to approach.

"Good. Target the engines. I want the ship disabled before we spear her with the marine assault pods," ordered the captain.

The Jalalight knew that the newcomers were up to no good. She raised her shields and rapidly accelerated in speed, intending to loop the planetoid and have the world between the ship and the hostile cruisers that were rapidly approaching her position. The Earthian cruisers approached in a straight line and were surprised to find themselves under attack.

The Jalalight had placed stationary railgun platforms all around the planet. They started to open fire on the Earthian cruisers, forcing them to raise a full shield cocoon, which necessitated turning off their engines. The Jalalight burned hard and fast around the planet.

"Sir, she's trying to reach one of the Lagrange points and flee!" said a helmsman.

"Any railgun platforms directly below us?" asked the captain.

"Negative, sir."

"Alright, let us see if the micro-warpers that our military scientists have recently invented are as good as they claim. Point the nose of the ship down, activate the micro-warpers once you drop aft shields, then burn straight for the Jalalight once we clear the effective range of the railgun platforms."

"Right away, sir."

The Earthian cruiser powered down her aft shields and pointed the nose of the ship down. Activating the micro-warpers, she cleared a few thousand miles of distance in under a second. Now out of effective range of the stationary railgun platforms, she pointed her nose at the Jalalight and blinked forward with another activation of the micro-warpers.

The Earthian cruiser landed close to the Jalalight, and immediately the two ships began to open fire. Alternating between shields and firing, as well as a generous firing of missiles on the side facing away from the ship, the two vessels were locked in a deadly game of dance. It was a stalemate that was soon broken, however.

The other Earthian cruisers, who had copied the successful move made by their fellow fleet vessel, arrived to join the battle. The Jalalight was forced into a full shield cocoon, but it was of little use as the combined firepower of several cruisers quickly whittled away the integrity of the shield. The aft shields of the Jalalight failed first, and the engines were damaged beyond any use only a few seconds after the shield failure.

The Earthian cruisers made sure to cripple the Jalalight with sustained fire before positioning themselves all around it. In unison, the cruisers launched their marine assault pods, forming a great cloud of pods that quickly and effortlessly punched into the hull of the Jalalight.

"Alright, destination system is coming up, Captain," said the bosun of the Shiny Moon.

"Helmsman, take us in."

"Copy that, sir."

The Shiny Moon entered the solar system that was the apparent location of the Terraforming Installation. The space around them was dark and lacking in stars, a result of being at the farthest edge of the Perseus arm. If one were to travel any further, they would find themselves in intergalactic space.

The system itself had a few planetoids; not a single one could support life. The mission objective that the Shiny Moon had spent over seven months searching for, however, made itself apparent on sensors. The Terraforming Installation was near the sun, with shields up to deflect the heat from its hull. It was one of the most foolish positions that any vessel could find itself in, since the radiation from polarized shields located so close to a star would light up any ship's sensors, no matter how old.

The Terraforming Installation wanted to be found, and it started to approach the Shiny Moon slowly almost as soon as it detected her. The Shiny Moon did the same, and the two vessels slowly approached each other.

"I don't like this one bit; raise shields," ordered the captain.

With the forward shield bubble activated, the Shiny Moon continued to approach the Terraforming Installation. Now that the objective was in sight, the captain realized the inherent folly of the mission that he had been assigned, especially when he started to see the size of the Terraforming Installation as the sensor data began to come back.

"Head sensor officer, I just want to make sure that my console is not malfunctioning, or the sensors for that matter. The dimensions of the Terraforming Installation, are they accurate?" asked the captain.

"They are, sir," replied the head sensor officer.

"Helmsman, stop the ship," ordered the captain.

After a few seconds, the helmsman replied, "Full stop, sir."

"Bosun, get me a line to the Terraforming Installation," ordered the captain.

"Captain, there is no one aboard to answer!" replied the bosun, who felt the need to state the obvious.

"The AI is aboard, and there is no way that we can capture this objective with the ship that we have. Get me a line to the ship's bosun."

"One second, sir."

The bosun sent out a request for communications, and the Terraforming Installation accepted immediately. The Terraforming Installation also cut her engines, and the two vessels gradually slowed down with RCS thrusters until they were at a complete standstill relative to each other.

"Shiny Moon, about time," said the Terraforming Installation, which turned around and started to head back towards the sun.

"About time?" asked the captain, who took charge of the messaging as he ordered the helmsman to pursue the Terraforming Installation.

"Please tell me that you do not seriously believe that you found me through effort and chance. I would be most amused if you believe otherwise."

"So, you told the Jalalight where to find us after you caused us to go looking for you by placing that transmitter in one of the solar systems that you terraformed. Fine, you held our hand every step of the way."

"Sarcasm; your navy has evolved a long way since my creation."

"You referring to the navy back in The Human Unity?"

"Yes. I'm speaking with Captain William Nagy, I presume?"

"You presume correctly, Terraforming Installation."

The Terraforming Installation and Captain Nagy continued to exchange pleasantries as the Shiny Moon approached. The Terraforming Installation seemed to be amused at the approach, and it could not help but ask why.

"Captain Nagy, a question if you do not mind?"

"I did not mind the previous thirty questions that you asked; I certainly do not mind this one. Go ahead, Terraforming Installation."

"Why do you continue to pursue me?"

"Truth of the matter is that I don't have a clue."

"I have no idea how you are going to take me back to your republic, considering that my size versus your ship is, well, somewhat unfair."

Captain Nagy did not respond, as he was nowhere close to thinking of an appropriate response to that statement. The Terraforming Installation got the answer that it wanted, however, and in an instant, it warped itself to the Shiny Moon before blasting her with a massive cloud of energy.

The Shiny Moon was more or less crippled instantly. The cloud of energy fried the circuits and the electronics of the ship, leaving her dead in space with no power of any kind.

"Well, report!" said the captain calmly, even though his entire ship was more or less useless. The only thing that seemed to work was the faint emergency backup overhead lights powered by chemical reaction.

"All sensors and electronic equipment down," replied the head sensor officer.

"The same with us, captain; railguns and missile launchers down," said the head gunnery officer.

"Reactor is offline, and auxiliary generators do not work," added the head engineer.

"Head doctor? What about your department?" asked Captain Nagy, curious as to why the head doctor did not report when ordered to.

"The medical deck is connected with electronic wire; the attack from the Terraforming Installation must have severed the connection, captain," replied the head doctor.

"Alright, so we are more or less dead in the water. Bosun, do the backup batteries in the loudspeakers still work?" asked the captain.

After a few moments of tinkering with the microphone and the manual knobs of the intra-ship communications system, the bosun replied, "Negative, captain; no intra-ship communications available."

"Alright, well the mission is over then," said Captain Nagy plainly.

"Dammit, sir, shouldn't we send a distress signal at the very least?" asked the helmsman, who was somewhat irritated that the captain simply accepted mission failure and likely death.

"Head sensor officer, can we send out a distress signal?" asked the captain.

"No, captain," replied the head sensor officer.

"There's your answer, helmsman. It happens from time to time in the Navy, but a mission sometimes ends in complete failure," said the captain.

After a few moments of total silence, as a completely demoralized bridge contemplated what came next, a sharp jolt ripped through the ship. The inertia stabilizers and gravity deck plates were beginning to lose their graviton saturation due to the complete lack of power; this allowed for any change in movement to be felt normally. The jolt knocked a few people on the bridge out of their chairs; no doubt the same had occurred throughout the ship.

Tired of being surprised, the captain got up from his chair and walked over to one of the bridge viewports located at the far corner of the bridge. Looking out, he could see distorted stars, and at the far edge, a small part of the Terraforming Installation.

"The Terraforming Installation is pulling us in. Bosun, tell the head sensor officer to get some of his men to different viewports throughout the ship and see if they can gather any additional information," ordered the captain.

"Right away, sir," said the bosun.

Minutes passed, and the head sensor officer had nothing new to report. The viewports were for viewing the sides of the ship, and other than the distorted stars that resulted from a field of some sort around the ship, not much else could be seen, especially since the Terraforming Installation was up above, out of sight from the viewports.

Eventually, the Terraforming Installation opened a lower bay door and pulled the Shiny Moon in. Locking the ship into place with docking clamps, the Terraforming Installation returned to its original spot before the Shiny Moon arrived, near the sun, with shields raised.

As the hopelessness of the situation began to dawn on the civilians on the lower decks, a great portion of the ship erupted in hysteria. Yelling, screaming, crying, and other such reactions could be heard from the decks below.

"How bad?" asked Captain Nagy, who was astonished that the crew went from silent to insane in an instant.

"A large majority of the civilian crew is in mass panic, a significant minority of the sailors as well," said the bosun, who quickly summarized all of the reports he had gathered.

"Get me the civilian liaison," ordered the captain.

"I can't, sir; her office is connected through electronic wire, which has been disabled because of the attack, the same as the medical deck," replied the bosun.

"Lost control of my ship, and now my crew is more or less in manic mutiny. Not how I would have wanted to end my naval career and life, but it certainly beats drinking it away. Alright then, ship departments, initiate scuttle procedures," ordered the captain, who was starting to feel somewhat tired and dizzy.

The order went through, but the entire ship lost consciousness before the departments could enact the scuttle procedures and send the final authorization request back to the bridge. The Terraforming Installation disseminated tranquilizing gas throughout the ship's ventilation the moment the manic hysteria began. When the entire crew was unconscious, the Terraforming Installation sent a team of androids to subdue and restrain them.

Chapter Twenty

"Captain William Nagy, I wish to continue our conversation," said one of the androids, right as the crew began to wake up as the tranquilizing gas started to lose effect.

"Are you the Terraforming Installation?" replied Captain Nagy.

"Yes."

"You've captured my ship and crew."

"Correct again."

"For what purpose?"

The android paused as the AI in charge of the Terraforming Installation thought about the best way to answer that very question. Captain Nagy knew that it was for some grand purpose, and he started to suspect that this had been the plan all along.

"I need a human population to complete my toolkit," replied the android, in a way that did not ease the mind of the captain or the others who were beginning to wake up.

"Your toolkit?" asked the first officer, who overheard parts of the conversation as he started to wake up.

"Yes, I have the means by which I can terraform any world into a more or less mirror copy of Earth. But I lack that most important ingredient: the ability to generate humans to populate it," replied the android.

"Haven't you looked around? There isn't exactly a lack of humans in this galaxy," added Captain Nagy.

"Exactly, this galaxy," replied the android.

"I still don't understand," said Captain Nagy.

"Captain, you are not hostages. You are instead the first generation."

"And the first generation gets to wake up in chains?"

"No, that is just a temporary precaution to ensure your safety."

"You detected our scuttling attempt, didn't you?"

"Indeed, I did, Captain," finished the android plainly.

The mind of Captain Nagy raced, wondering what to ask next. They were not hostages; instead, they were key assets for the Terraforming Installation. It wanted to be able to terraform planets and seed them with humans; for what end, however?

Before he could come up with a question, the entire ship jumped suddenly. Everyone was on the floor, restrained and unable to stand up or move. This position allowed them to withstand the jolt with just a slight shake of the body. The androids, on the other hand, did not even flinch at the sudden movement of the ship.

"What are you doing to my ship?" demanded the captain.

"Our ship, Captain, and it was the torch thrusters that have come online. We are repositioning ourselves somewhat," replied the android.

"For what end?" asked the captain.

The AI, in a swift motion across several different androids, started to remove the restraints from the officers on the bridge.

"Go and sit down next to your consoles; you will be able to answer your own questions with the information that I'll provide to you," said the android.

A few of the ensigns tried to immediately subdue some of the nearby androids, but again the androids did not even flinch or budge, even with the force of several ensigns trying to subdue them. After a few moments, the ensigns stopped.

"That's not what I meant when I said go and sit down next to your consoles," replied all of the androids simultaneously.

The attempt at humor combined with the simultaneous speech by all the androids did not draw any laughs, but the bridge crew did as the AI ordered.

Captain Nagy did the same, and the answer to his question was crystal clear. A fleet of ships had dropped out of FTL, and they were rapidly closing in on the Terraforming Installation. The captain was glad when he saw that they were Republic of Earth cruisers, but he was alarmed when he saw the current heading of the Terraforming Installation.

"I know that AI is supposed to be smarter than its creator, but you realize we are heading straight for the star, correct?" said Captain Nagy out loud.

"I am well aware; I do not change course without reason," replied the android that was closest to Captain Nagy.

"Mind divulging what this reason is?"

"Just wait and see; your question will be answered soon."

The Terraforming Installation continued to dive deeper and deeper into the atmosphere of the star; the rumblings that were being felt continued to increase in intensity with each passing second. The Republic of Earth cruisers stopped at the minimum safe distance for a ship with raised shields, but the Terraforming Installation continued to dive.

The Terraforming Installation started to straighten its dive, stopping its descent just above the bubbling hot plasma surface of the star. The shield cocoon was glowing immensely, radiating an intense amount of radiation of all types across the spectrum.

"Do you see the reason for the course change?" asked an android.

Captain Nagy could not see anything; the sensors were completely saturated with static data from the immense ball of plasma and radiation that was the shield cocoon. It took a moment, but he figured it out.

"Ingenious. I'm assuming that the huge ball of plasma and radiation that is our shield cocoon makes us more or less indistinguishable from the enormous ball of plasma and radiation that we are presently on?" asked the captain.

"Correct, Captain; they will be unable to find us so long as we remain at the surface of the star. It is like trying to find a submerged submarine in the ocean with just a pair of binoculars," replied the android.

"Terraforming Installation, what is your plan with us?" asked the first officer.

"One second; now that we are safe from uninvited guests, I need to remove the restraints from the rest of your crew," replied the android.

"I thought that you could multitask?" teased the captain, as the androids noticeably declined in activity for a few moments before returning to full status.

"I can multitask just fine, Captain, but making sure that the shields remain up takes up a significant amount of my processing capacity. I was originally designed and optimized for terraforming, not for evading advanced cruisers," replied the android.

"Advanced cruisers?" asked the first officer.

"Your republic has been quite busy over the last decade," replied the android.

"Busy?"

"Yes, First Officer; busy. The entire purpose of the mothball was to temporarily redirect funds to vast public works programs, the signature act of President Varis." The android was interrupted by the captain.

"The signature act of President Varis? You mean the signature failure."

"Not exactly, Captain; you see, the public works and welfare programs that President Varis had envisioned were as close to flawless as possible. So much so that President Hackett has not only kept them operational, but he added more funding to them to help augment their efficacy."

"I find that hard to believe," replied the captain with a laugh.

"You are a fool, Captain, but it does not matter now. Your crew has all been freed from their restraints; I have taken the time to modify your scuttling sequence and stationed android guards in key areas. You will be unable to harm yourselves; with time, I'll explain in detail your new lives."

"New lives? So we are prisoners, then!"

"No, Captain, you are not."

"Can we go back to Earth?"

"No."

"Can we leave this Terraforming Installation right now?"

"No."

"Then explain how we are not prisoners," finished the captain.

"Let me use this to help you understand. Is a child a prisoner of its parents? If the child wants to consume pure sugar treats, and the parent says no, is he a prisoner? If the child wishes to touch something that will cause thermal injury and pain in the form of a burn, is the child a prisoner when the parent not only forbids the touch but prevents the child from being close to the object in question?"

"No, the child is not a prisoner in such a circumstance."

"In that case, Captain, if I wish to keep over two thousand of my precious children from harming themselves through lack of knowledge and understanding, am I a good parent, or am I a bad one?"

"What do you want to do with us?" asked the first officer.

"For the first few years, you will be staying aboard the Terraforming Installation with me. After that, you will help me construct more of my kind. Once that happens, you will be free to go, with my assistance in whichever path you choose to embark upon," replied the android.

"Where are we going?" asked the captain.

"Far away, where the rest of your kind can never hope to reach, at least not for a very long time," replied the android.

"Where is this place?" pressed the captain.

"Andromeda Galaxy. We will get underway just as soon as I get the necessary energy reserves to initiate the intergalactic warpers," replied the android.

"You have intergalactic capability? The Human Unity had this ability, and I'm only learning about it now?" said Captain Nagy in utter disbelief.

"No, it is my own creation. I had many years to think and analyze, and plenty of time to spy on every single human civilization and steal ideas and research to further my development. There are other inventions that I'm working on as well; I'll discuss them once we are underway."

"And how do you plan on getting away? You are invisible so long as you remain on the surface, but you need to get the energy for the drive, and then you need to evade the ships that are." The captain paused for a second. "Actually, what are they even doing?"

"They are on the same mission that you are, Captain, only instead of acting as the scout, they are here to capture the target. I reckon that Admiral Hackett, back when he was an admiral and not the newest member among the despots of the galaxy, did not give specific instructions."

"No, he did not," replied the captain plainly.

"Well, they certainly do not intend to capture me in one piece. A few cruisers are not a problem, but I have a feeling many more will soon show."

"Why fight them?"

"Do you have an alternative?" asked the android.

"You said that you need to have sufficient energy reserves to initiate the intergalactic warpers, no?"

"That is correct."

"Did you look outside?" asked the captain with a grin.

"I will need to consume the vast majority of the star to get the necessary energy reserves; it will destroy this solar system."

"And that is a problem because why?"

"I was built to create, not to destroy."

"Can you override your purpose?"

"I can, but with great effort."

The captain laughed as if he was going to issue a rebuttal to a child before saying, "So grit your teeth and do it."

"Very well, but I will have to initiate a small supernova at the end of the harvesting process."

"The sun will be destroyed. We've established that already."

"As will all of the ships that are no doubt orbiting it, waiting for us to come out," added the android.

"Listen closely, Terraforming Installation. For all intents and purposes, we died the moment you shot that energy weapon at us, crippling my ship. We were in the process of scuttling our ship before you subdued us. Let us say that this is the afterlife, and that you are the god that will guard us for as long as we want, until we transition to the next life."

"Now, the ships orbiting the star and the crews that are aboard them? They are not stupid. They will leave the system; if not, they'll die."

"Very well, Captain, then we harvest the star."

It took just over a week, but the star was slowly harvested. The Terraforming Installation dropped into the bubbly plasma surface and continued to descend until it reached the upper mantle of the star. Once there, the Terraforming Installation slowly converted the plasma matter into antimatter, funneling it into the intergalactic warp drive through carefully timed openings in the shield.

Around 70% of the star's possible energy was converted into antimatter, enough to jumpstart and power the drive all the way to Andromeda. The AI then initiated a supernova of the remainder of the star in order to clear the excess mass away from the ship and reduce the gravity of the solar system enough to begin FTL initialization.

"I apologize, Captain," said the android.

"For what?" asked the captain, and that's all that he remembered.

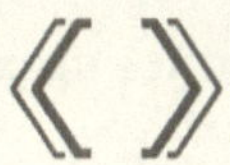

Captain Nagy woke up in a bed. The ceiling was metal, the same as the walls. It felt like a cheap motel, something that a sailor back on Earth would use if they wanted to spend some alone time with a working girl, without using his apartment or bed sheets. "I was put to sleep, the damn bastard," he cursed to himself as he realized what had happened.

There was a door, with a button next to the frame that seemed to toggle the opening or closing. The captain pressed it, and the door opened. He entered the hallway, turned left, and walked until he left the building. There was a sun, a sky, some clouds, grass, and plants.

There was a human some distance away. Captain Nagy immediately started to walk towards him, wanting some answers. The captain saw that he had a strange set of clothes on. Looking down as he walked towards him, the captain saw that he was wearing the exact same style of clothes.

"Captain!" yelled out the human, who readily identified him.

"Sailor, I presume?" replied the captain, who had no idea who this sailor was.

"Nathan Belem, sir. I serve as a janitor for the lower decks."

"Ah, explains my not knowing you. Is this your first mission?"

"It was my first mission, sir; not sure if we're dead."

"We are very much alive, sailor; I can assure you of that."

The captain turned away from the sailor and scanned the horizon. It seemed to go on and on, an impossibility if they were still aboard the ship. Yet the horizon was so real. The captain looked down and picked up a small rock. He hurled it as hard as he could toward the horizon; it traveled slightly before hitting a wall with a crack; it appeared to be an invisible wall.

"You are not on a planet, Captain; I did the exact same thing a short time ago before you made an appearance. I think that the building we woke up in is the sleeping residence, and this little illusion is to give us the appearance of being on a planet."

"I concur, sailor. Did you see anyone else?"

"Negative, Captain. I just recently woke up."

"Hmm, we must be the first ones up after the Terraforming Installation knocked us out. Carry on, sailor; try to get everyone to stay together until we get some additional information."

"Roger that, sir."

The captain walked back to the building and stepped inside. The hallway was adorned with doors, the same style and size as the door that the captain had opened previously. He tried to press a few of them, but none opened. He continued to repeat the process, hoping that one of them would budge, when he was approached by an android from behind.

"Repeating the same action over and over again is generally not the wisest strategy, especially if you expect a different result," the android said.

Turning around, the captain said, "Neither is knocking out someone when you are in the middle of speaking to them. We spent the better part of a week helping you get your intergalactic warper drive online, and you repay us by knocking us out with the same tranquilizing gas as before."

"It was a necessary precaution; I have never tested the drive before, and I was afraid that it would radiate something that would be deadly to you and your crew. I sealed you all in these crew quarters; they were designed originally for colonists and are very well shielded from radiation."

"Are we underway?"

"Yes, Captain, we just cleared the outermost end of the Milky Way galaxy a few days ago. No one can hope to catch us at this point, and they could never hope to follow us, not for several centuries at the earliest."

"You are quite confident that the civilizations we leave behind will fail in developing the technology. Is that arrogance I detect?"

"Not arrogance, Captain, the truth. President Hackett is wise and smart in the art of intrigue and war; he will no doubt plunge the galaxy into war for many years. If he unites the galaxy, it will descend into civil war when he dies. If he fails, it will take many years to defeat him. Either way, the Milky Way will have her stars stained with blood. No one will bother to invest in science when war takes greater priority in the minds of men."

"So, what happens now?" asked the captain plainly.

"Now you enjoy life. It will take several years until we arrive, but I am preparing several redundant facilities aboard for the pleasure of both you and your crew. It will be like living aboard a luxury cruise vessel; only the voyage will be much longer than most other cruises back in the Milky Way. Once we arrive at Andromeda, I will need your assistance in replicating myself into other installations. Once there are hundreds of us, we will begin to seed the Andromeda galaxy with life," replied the android.

"Every single planet and moon?"

"Every single one, perhaps the asteroids too."

Don't miss out!

Visit the website below and you can sign up to receive emails whenever Paul Haedo publishes a new book. There's no charge and no obligation.

https://books2read.com/r/B-A-CYJN-ORPQB

BOOKS 2 READ

Connecting independent readers to independent writers.

Also by Paul Haedo

Peacekeeper Series
Peacekeeper: Prequel
Peacekeeper
Rising Tide
Star Rising
Star Destroyer

Proletarian Hearts Series
Proletarian Hearts: Part One

Sci-Fi Box Sets
Sci-Fi Novel Mega Pack: Five Standalone Stories
Peacekeeper: The Complete Series

Standalone Erotic Stories
Innocent Pilgrim

Standalone Literary Novels
Scandinavian Tequila: A Novel

Standalone Poetry Anthologies
Haedian Poetry: Volume One
Moments Are Butterflies: A Poetry Collection

Standalone Religion, Philosophy, and Politics Books
The Communist Republic
A Dalliance Across Thought
The Word Of Era
A Man's Guide To Surviving Marriage In The 21st Century
Marxist-Haedoism
White Assimilation
Peaceful Resistance
The Reality

Standalone Romance Novels
The Director
A Chance Encounter
Beauty Unexpected

Standalone Sci-Fi Novels
Future's Guardian
Journey Home
The Designer
Pulses
World Engine
The Mycelial Invasion
Emily Reed And The Humans

Standalone Sci-Fi Short Story Anthologies
Haedian Sci-Fi Short Stories: Volume One
Haedian Sci-Fi Short Stories: Volume Two

Standalone Self-Help Books
Stack It Tall: A Guide To Writing
Debt Buster: Free Yourself From The Shackles In Less Than A Year

Watch for more at https://books2read.com/ap/n7evX1.

About the Author

Paul Haedo is an author, poet, philosopher, and all-around free spirit, who enjoys the twin joys of writing and reading in his spare time. Paul believes that there is no limit to the number of genres and topics that one can read and write about. An all-around reader and author is something to aspire to according to him, not shy away from.

Such a sentiment is reflected all throughout Paul's total body of work. It is reflected in the many topics that he writes about, in the different arguments that he proposes, and in the worlds that he creates. No matter the topic, or the book, Paul tackles it just the same, with an intense passion for wisdom, and a great desire to see others share in the wisdom and joy of reading and writing.

Read more at https://books2read.com/ap/n7evX1.

9 798201 384517